Shadow Venom

Jeremiah Anderson

Shadow Venom

By Jeremiah Anderson

Jeremiah Anderson

Shadow Venom

Copyright © 2024 by Jeremiah Anderson

Hunter is a fifteen-year-old boy who wants nothing more than a happy life with his father and best friend, Ben, but his life is forever changed when his father is killed by Russian Terrorists. So, Hunter fought back, and he would like nothing more than to get revenge. Then, Hunter begins to see that recent events have changed him. His anger, hatred, and fear are at the core of everything he is now. Will things ever be the same?

First paperback edition July 2024

ISBN: 979-8-218-46370-0

"Always focus on saving those you care about rather than destroying those you hate."

-Jeremiah Anderson

Shadow Venom

~

Thank you for being there for me and helping me

believe that I could do this. This first one's for you

Gabe.

~

Shadow Venom

Prologue

I wake up, and I'm back in the forests of New York. Adrick is running for me. I look behind me to see if I have a clear path to run, but I do not; the forest that surrounds me is covered by thorn bushes, and the trees have unnatural spikes coming out of them. Pulling out my gun to shoot Adrick, I squeeze the trigger, and nothing comes out; my magazine is empty. I lift my arm to use my flame emitter to roast him alive, but it's jammed nothing comes out. My electrified venom shocker breaks away on my arm and rusts away into the gentle breeze. Adrick moves closer and closer by the second. I reach behind my back for my shield, but it isn't there, nor are my daggers or katana. I panic as he gets closer. I lift a stick from the ground to throw at him, but he's invincible; he smashes every tree he comes across, chips of wood flying everywhere.

Bracing myself for the impact, I turn my head while placing my arms over my chest to protect any vital organs. But with his strength, he would destroy me. I don't run since I couldn't outrun him if I tried. Adrick grabs a tree with his bare hands and lifts it above his head, throwing it to the ground and smashing it into trillions of pieces. The shards of wood fly at me, cutting my arms. But they don't seem to hurt. I figure the adrenaline must be preventing me from feeling it. I block as many as I can by covering my face with my arms.

Once I look between my arms, Adrick stands there in front of me, looking down upon me like some rodent he caught in a trap, which he did since I have no escape. I close my eyes gently hoping it will be quick, but he grabs my throat and lifts me against the tree, the spikes stab into my back, but still no pain.

Blood dripping from Adrick's chest, from where I stabbed him. I almost consider apologizing, but that wouldn't be nearly enough.

He looks at me with those evil eyes. "Wake up!" Wake up? What does he mean? "Wake up! Hunter!" How does he know my name?

Jeremiah Anderson

Part 1

"The Genesis."

Chapter 1

I lie down on Long Beach, feeling the hot sun on my face and the sand between my toes. It feels nice, everything feels perfect, it's like if this moment froze forever, then I would happily live in it.

My happy moment was ruined when Matthew and Markus kicked sand in my eyes. I get up in frustration, holding a fistful of sand. But before I make any move to throw it at them, I spot them over at the volleyball net waving me over. I gladly join them. I'm not good at volleyball, nor do I understand how to play the game. But I'm competitive and I don't back down from a challenge, so I play anyway.

Our games usually go on for a long time, so I often lose track of time. But today is different, I've something exciting planned for today at noon. The game ends when Markus hits the ball into the ocean. We are at least one hundred feet away, yet he still manages to get it in. No one wants to go into the ocean anymore since rumors started being spread that Russians are secretly setting bases up along the coast of Long Beach. They believed that a small group of Russian soldiers wanted to attack while the rest did not, so they went into America as a rogue team of terrorists. I don't believe in that stuff.

I grab my things and head to the parking lot for my motorcycle. I've had it for years, but I refuse any type of change. So, I've never even considered getting rid of it. It took a couple of tries but I eventually got my motorcycle to roar, the sound it makes when it starts up. The metallic paint on the motorcycle, along with the worn flames give it this old look. Which makes sense because it is quite old being my fathers before me. He used to ride on it during his childhood. So, one day out of the blue. He gave me this broken-down motorcycle. It doesn't seem to look like much, but it means the world to me.

The ride isn't the comfiest but when I reach Forest Hills, I freeze with its beauty. It might look old and torn down to some people, but to me it's everything. After riding through the town and stopping by and waving to some of the kids from school, I head straight for home.

Jeremiah Anderson

I look up to see dark grey clouds, sending a chill up my spine that breathes cold air on my shoulder. Pulling into the driveway I turn to park alongside next to the garage. My father's cop car is inside, and I don't want to damage it. I open the garage door to work on a few of my projects before my special plan is ready.

Pulling up a chair to my private section of the garage I lift my shield onto the desk. It has a thick layer of glass and various metals on the inside to withstand bullet fire. I try to shine the shield as best I can, so it's not only functional but so it looks cool as well. I slide my tote out with all my hand weapons. I pull out my katana that must be sharpened all the time to keep it nice and shiny. Along with boots that have daggers on the sides of them. I don't enjoy having knives on my hips because if I fall that doesn't feel good. So, placing them on my boots was a compromise. Minus the fact that they are illegal in most states

I lift my guns out of the tote to work on their barrels. I have nearly accomplished my work on creating a silent gun. I tweak it slightly every day so I can make it that much more silent. I look to see if there is anything else, and I nearly miss my favorite weapon. My clawed gloves. I have attached razor-sharp blades to the ends of these high-durability gloves. After countless nights

Shadow Venom

I have finally figured out a way to make them retract whenever I want to make a fist, so I don't stab myself. I open a drawer in front of me to pull out my goggles, that have thermal sensory on them. So, I can practically see through walls.

Finally, one of my most deadly weapons is my flame emitter. I attach it to my right arm and use my left hand to press the button on the top of it to turn on the flame emitter. I prefer it not to be one-handed use since I don't want the system to break on me and burn the house down. I fill it with butane since it's the best choice liquid to use in the flame emitter.

I tried to refill the flame emitter, but before I could get the cartridge in, I heard the doorbell ring. I checked my watch to see the time, and it was exactly noon. I rushed for the door and opened it to see what I had planned, standing there waiting for me. Standing there is my best friend Ben Wilde, with brown hair that follows the shape of his face to his neck. He is tall in stature and very strong as well but isn't quite as fast as I am. His demeanor is kind and benign, and he seems to always be so sure of every action that he does.

He looks at me with the same goofy smile that I've seen a million times before. "Ready to lose Mr. Hunter Conners?" he asks jokingly.

Jeremiah Anderson

"I'll never lose," I reply. He stands there holding his gaming system in his hands anxiously waiting for me to let him in. But when I open the door enough to let him through, my father walks out the door over to the minivan that awaits him, with Ben's father inside. Mr. Damien Wilde. He has a uniform haircut with a soft beard that wraps around his sturdy jaw and over his lip.

Ben's father, Mr. Damien, is an ex-convict. He used to be an assassin who was hired to kill people around the world, but at one point one of his jobs was a trick, and he got captured. He was put in prison for quite a few years and during that time my father was assigned as his guard. They got to know each other and became friends. At some point, he was released on good behavior. He and my father continued to hang out and became close friends. Not long after, my father introduced him to Ben's mother, an aspiring actress. They eventually got married and lived happily together.

My father has done so much for our community, helped so many people, and saved so many lives that I'm worried that one day there will be a fight he doesn't win, and that he won't make it home in time for dinner. But I live in the hope that that never happens. Plus, he is going on patrol with an assassin so I'm sure he'd be just fine in any situation.

Shadow Venom

Mr. Damien waves Ben and me off as they pull out of the driveway and head for Long Beach, the exact place I just came from. I generally miss my father when he's away, but Ben manages to keep me busy. I hook up the gaming system to the television so we can play games, while my mother brings in freshly baked cookies. No matter what anyone else says, my mother is the best cook ever, and I wouldn't trade her for the world. However, she does worry a lot about me and was mortified when I scraped my knee. I was four. I'm her only child so I'm the baby of the family technically.

Ben and I play video games for a little while until we get tired and turn on the news before heading to the kitchen to grab a few more cookies. My mother, Ben, and I chat in the kitchen for a little while about who would win in a fight. My father or Bens. Everyone knows Ben's would win. But I like to say stuff like my father has the entire police force on his side. Though Mr. Damien could probably win a fight against all the police, and not even break a sweat. He's incredibly strong and can bench press 1,000 pounds and run a mile in about 3 minutes. He's in peak physical condition.

I walk back into the living room with Ben. He plops back down on the couch holding his controller in his hand as I bend down under the television to start the gaming system up. "I bet I'll win this time. Just like all the other times," I say, expecting a funny reply from Ben. When I turn to look at him, his eyes are glued to the television. His face is white with fear, I wonder what it could be, so I get up to sit down next to him to watch the news.

I look at the screen for a few moments before noticing that there has been an explosion, it's huge. There's a lot of them. Spread out, and they're centered in one place. Long Beach. The very place my father is at, I don't believe this. He isn't dead, maybe he's not there yet, is what I try to tell myself. But then faces flash across the screen. I see many of my father's coworkers, everything feels okay until my father's face is front and center on the screen, followed by Ben's father.

A news reporter flies above the scene of the attack. "The attack is confirmed to be by a group of terrorists, presumed to be Russian threats. They refuse to show America mercy. That is all the information we can share at this time," the woman tries to hold back tears as she gets the final sentence out. So, the rumors are true, evil Russians are trying to take down America.

I try to stand but I can't even form a word, I begin to choke on air, I can't breathe. I use all my strength to stand. I wander over to the stairs but barely make it up the first step before falling again. My worst fear has come to life, and I can't do anything about it.

Can I?

A thought comes across my head, I have the weapons, the equipment, the knowledge. I can get revenge on them. My breathing slows. My thoughts turn dark. Everything slows as I black out from the fear and anger that enters my head and heart.

I must kill them… all of them. Nothing but darkness and evil is in my heart at this moment, the darkest moment of my life.

Will anyone survive my wrath?

Chapter 2

Hours have passed by from the moment that would change my life forever. I have spent most of that time in my garage finishing my inventions that will soon be used for deadly combat purposes.

I have finished constructing a special combat suit, that I have designed using my motorcycle protective vest and my father's police gear. I also decided to add my dagger boots and my shield as well. I painted the shield midnight black, so the metallic silver wouldn't give me away. I also added two holsters, both unevenly distributed on my legs, one closer to my knee on the left and the other closer to my hip on the right. I wanted something more just for fear, so I decided to add my katana.

I was unsure about adding my flame emitter at first, but I decided to because it would be a formidable weapon against my enemies. My final weapon choice will be my clawed glove since they are weapons that will allow me to kill my enemies with the slightest of ease, and I will be able to kill people without making a sound.

As I'm about to walk out a white marker catches my eye. I will need a name, a name that will strike fear into people's hearts. I pick up the marker and at the top right armor plate in bold letters, I write, "SHADOW VENOM." In the case that someone recognizes me, I take a ski mask with me to conceal myself. I wear my goggles over my mask so I can conceal my eye color and so I will be able to see in the dark.

I have one more gadget that isn't quite ready yet but will be extremely helpful later. But without it working properly it would be too dangerous to even consider taking it out into the field.

Running up the stairs, hoping my mother won't see me, I pack a bag with everything I will be using and gather food and water for when I'm done. I walk downstairs and find many of the neighborhood moms gathered in my living room grieving for my mother. I attempt to get out of the vicinity as quickly as possible before they offer to have me join. I just head outside and fill up the gas in my motorcycle.

Jeremiah Anderson

Once I was finished, I decided that I didn't want to walk through all that again. So I climbed a tree outside of my house and jumped onto the window ledge to climb through the window. With me having years of self-defense training I have gained much more strength than most people my age, with me being only fifteen. Ben takes the class too. He is excellent at sparring and one of the best in the class. Which has inspired me to put my black belt on my suit as well.

My mother has gone to bed at this point, I have decided that this is the time to sneak out and get revenge on the Russians. I take my motorcycle down the road a couple of blocks, so I don't risk waking my mother or too many neighbors. It takes a couple of tries to get the roar out but it's ever so satisfying once it does start up.

~

I ride until I reach the edge of the forest near Long Beach. I dress myself in my suit and make sure I have all my needed equipment. I tread lightly through the forest using my thermal ray goggles when needed.

Bam! I heard off in the distance. At first, I wondered if they had found me already, before I jumped for the attack, I noticed two soldiers firing shots around a campfire. I decided to start with my main weapon, my claw gloves, to see how well they do in combat.

Jumping out of the darkness I shocked one soldier causing him to point his gun at me. But before he could pull the trigger, I shoved his hand away, and I slit his throat with my claws. I bend down to slit the other soldier's thigh from behind him making him fall onto the ground unaware of the cause of his pain. I pulled my hand back and stabbed my claws deep into his throat. For a moment I almost feel appalled by what I had done but moments later I have no regrets, for these men contributed to the murder of my father.

I quietly sneak over to the campfire of my next victims this time using my daggers. I stab two of the soldiers in their hearts and finish by slitting the throat of the third Russian man.

Moving from one campfire to the next I slowly begin to realize more of my true nature, and how strong I truly can be.

Reaching the final campfire, I decided to use my shield and flame emitter. I swept the leg of a soldier causing him to fall. The other soldier hears what has happened and immediately looks at the man on the ground. Jumping out of the darkness I deflect his bullets with my shield then place one hand on the emitter to activate it roasting the soldiers to death.

I take a quick look around and notice that I have taken out all the campfires of soldiers. I needed some way to blow this place up, so I picked up a few grenades from fallen soldiers. I arm myself with a gun in one hand and arm myself with my shield on the other, discreetly running towards the base. It appears to have a chain fence with barbwire at the top and two towers. I aim at one of the guards at the top of the tower where most could see him, and I shoot him in the head causing him to fall to the ground.

A siren cries alerting all the soldiers of me, but I don't mind.

A group comes from around the side and fires upon me, but I block with my shield and end up taking them out before they can land a hit on me. Soldiers come around from the other side and try to attack me with swords, so I decided to have a little fun and pull out my katana. They attempted numerous attacks on me, but I gave them a one-way ticket to heaven before I could return the favor. A soldier from above gets a grenade ready to throw but before he can get it to leave his hands, I shoot him right between the eyes. He hits the ground next to the tower causing the grenade to blow up the tower, helpful but not my goal. I quickly unclip a grenade from my belt aiming for the explosives in the base throwing it over the fence, I almost freeze with a feeling of completion as I see the grenade contacting the explosives. But this thing isn't over yet.

I come to my senses after I realize that I'm running in the opposite direction of the explosion before I get killed. Diving for the ground I get my head caught into a bush but it's better than being blown to pieces like my father.

I trail back around the base afterward and discover a few badly wounded soldiers and decide to leave them because it would be mercy to simply kill them. I picked up the least wounded soldier and tied him up with rope to carry on my motorcycle. When I reached my motorcycle, I went a few more yards and made it to the bridge. I untied the man and put him into a chair that I found lying on the side of the road. I stab my claws into his side to get him talking.

I hold the position for a couple of seconds, so he knows I'm not messing around. "Are there any more bases?" I ask in a deep voice. I prefer them to fear me since my voice isn't anything to be afraid of.

Jeremiah Anderson

A few tears drip down the man's face. "I don't know…. I." He tries to force words out, but he wheezes and is having a hard time breathing. He won't be of any use to me. I tie him even tighter to the chair to reassure him he doesn't escape. Gently tipping the chair back against the railing on the bridge, I grab the legs of the chair and flip it off the edge of the bridge. Sending the man to the bottom of the river below.

I take off my suit and clean my knives before starting up my motorcycle and riding off back home. I pull up next to the side of my garage and throw my bag over my shoulder so I can climb up the tree and reach my windowsill. Once settled I head off to bed.

~

Getting only a quarter of a night's rest I feel a little sleep-deprived, but I'll manage to get along through the day without it.

I head off to school for the day to take my mind off what's happened. The teachers have decided to cut some classes so kids can get home and stay safe while this whole Russian attack is taking place.

I stop by my friend Chloe Kooper's locker, put my shoulder on her locker, and simply say, "Hey," in a manly attractive voice to get her attention.

Shadow Venom

She shoots me a look but winds up blushing and giving me a small smile. Chloe, Ben, and I have been friends for years and have been best friends since we met. Ben and I both like her, so we compete to see who can win her over. We all know I did when I invited her to a school dance a few years back, but to keep the fun going I let Ben think that he had a chance.

I stare into her beautiful blue eyes trying not to get lost in them. "So, any plans for the weekend?" I ask.

"Other than making sure I don't get killed by a group of Russian terrorists, no not really," she says jokingly. She has the gift of making people smile in the darkest moments. I try to act like I didn't find what she said funny, but I can't help but smile. "Oh, that's right... I'm sorry about your father, Hunter." She says in a sorrowful tone.

"Eh, I'll manage." I attempt to hide my real feelings, but I can tell she sees right through me. I mean what else is to be expected of me? To just start balling and whining in the middle of school? I sure hope not. We continued down the hall until splitting up and going our separate ways, I headed to English followed by history and science. At lunch, I don't feel up to sitting in the cafeteria with the rest of my class, so I go backstage into the old announcements room to eat my lunch and figure out my next plan of action.

When the final bell of the day rings I dash to the electronics room where a group of kids will sell you pretty much any electrical object that they can get their hands on. I normally don't associate with this kind of stuff, but I need a special battery pack that is too expensive to buy from the store or online. They don't even seem to question why I want it they just give it to me. Before I could give him the money, the boy stared me in the eye. I feel nervous, unsure of what is happening.

He pushes my hand back towards my pocket. "For your father," the boy says refusing to make any more eye contact. He treats me as though I've disappeared.

"Thank you," I respond, I try to remain neutral, but I can't help but wonder why. Is there something more? I feel as though my father isn't the only reason for this. Plus, these guys never give out something like this for free. As I'm about to leave what appears to be the leader of their little crime syndicate walks in. As I'm leaving, I pause at the door to see the boy who gave me the battery being beaten by their ringleader. I considered going back

Shadow Venom

to help but I realized that I would only make it worse for him. Plus, I don't need to worry about other people.

I hop back onto my motorcycle and head off to where I work since I need the extra money for my mother. But halfway there I ran out of gas; I suppose I used up more gas than I thought yesterday. I stopped over by a nearby gas station but realized it was not the gas. It turns out the battery is dead. I have no other choice but to stop by the mechanics and walk the rest of the way. I walk along the side of the road feeling the sunshine down my face and arms, with the breeze of the wind gently blowing the trees, swaying them back and forth. A moment of relaxation, something I had not felt since before my father died. Which wasn't that long ago.

Turning the corner gives me a view of the local grocery store where I work as a bagger. I stand at the end of a register and bag until I'm tipped then I circulate throughout the line of other baggers. My usual pay is five to fifteen dollars per tip, only because I'm young and polite. The manager allows me to watch television while I bag, that is if I don't get too distracted. Most of the old people don't like it because they complain about how they had no television to watch at my age when they were working. Well, dirt didn't exist when they were my age either. I could care less about what they think because I'm here to make money not get life coaching advice.

While I'm bagging something catches my eye on the television. News reporters are flying over the different bases they've found in the forest. But most of the helicopters get taken out by a missile or shot down. I finish up bagging to head off back to the mechanics. I found my motorcycle battery replaced and ready for use. I could probably learn how to change one myself but that seems like something a father teaches a son and well. I'm not really in that situation anymore, am I?

Chapter 3

The moon shines brightly tonight. Riding through town at midnight, praying that I would not be seen, I continued to the wilderness. If my mother were to discover me, who knows how this could end? I do know that she wouldn't be very fond of it. After a little while of riding, I reached the edge of the forest. I conceal my motorcycle with large sticks and other plants, before heading out into the wilderness in search of my next base of victims. The underbrush of the forest tickles me even through the suit. I watch the full moon shine as it spreads its nightlight to all the creatures below. Owl's hoot and coyotes howl, but there isn't one sound that stops me from continuing my journey. I hear screams coming out of the forest. Are they American? I listen closer, to conclude that they are Russian screams. I can hear the explosion of grenades and the rain of fire from guns. I become more curious about the situation, so

Jeremiah Anderson

curious that I climb up a tree and look down onto the Russian base below. I see a huge group of Americans easily outnumbering the Russians taking them out one by one.

I gradually climb down the tree only about halfway, then I leap from branch to branch until I've almost reached the open field the base sits on. I look down to see a man below me who doesn't appear to be a Russian. I will use him as leverage. I drop from the tree taking him to the ground, wrapping my arm around his neck, holding a knife to his throat, and forcefully dragging him into the open field.

The man struggles to get free from my strong grip. "Help! Help! Help!" the man yells continuously until his companions notice and rush to his aid pointing their guns at me.

"Whoa, watch it, buddy," a man says rushing over trying to calm everyone down. "Would you like to explain what you are doing son?" he pulls down his bandana covering his long curly mustache. He's tall with orange hair covering most of his head. I've never trusted anyone with a mustache like that because they always seemed to look like some old-west bandit. One time when I was younger, I saw a new bus driver with that type of mustache, and I didn't trust him, so I walked to school and wound up showing up late. But I later found

34

out that, that man kidnapped the children on the bus and led them over and into a lake where they drowned.

I stand here ready to kill the man in my arm in case they try to kill me first. But I believe that I have far too much leverage for them to risk it. "Listen up boy, if you let him go, I will order my men to put their guns down, deal?" I simply nod complying with his wish. He seems agitated by what's happening but calm at the same time. "There now that that's over let's discuss the reason for this," he says trying to act as though he has complete control of the entire situation.

"I want to know why you people are here," I say sternly in hopes it will help me gain some authority.

"Okay, I'll go first. We are here to stop the Russian bases from spreading further into the country. At night we find a base and we take it out. We have had severe losses, but they will not be in vain because we will overcome the enemy in the end. We cannot receive help from the American military for a while because if they attack, the camps of hostages will be killed. But we can use all the help we can get." Everything he says is sincere, but I cannot join them. If I do, then they will risk ruining my plan.

Jeremiah Anderson

"As tempting as that offer is I'm going to have to refuse, I work alone so I have no worry about protecting other people and will not help or be helped by anyone," I say in a quick and aggressive tone.

He gives me a small nod accepting my refusal and offers me his hand. At first, I refused. Afraid he might try to kill me or worse. I shake his hand anyway since this man seems like he would make a good ally, and with his will to win, a formidable enemy. He shakes my hand sternly while slipping a card into the palm of my hand. Upon release, he gives me a quick salute before calling his men and retreating to where I assume the location of the next base is. Turning around to hike in the opposite direction, I headed off to search for another base, since they took out the base I was going for.

~

The trek goes on for hours until I finally decide to head back since I'm probably not going to find another base tonight and right when I'm about to turn back and head home I see the slight glare of a bonfire. I became curious about its reasoning for being here, so I chose to stay for now. Sneaking silently up to the fire, I hide in a bush just yards from it. A fence lining around a courtyard of what appears to be a small park. I see guards patrolling around the perimeter of the fence trying to protect whatever is inside.

Shadow Venom

Climbing up a tree for a better advantage point, I steadily walk across the branch overhanging the fence. Trying to stay as quiet as possible as I jump onto the nearby rooftop. I slide down a pillar landing on the ground, carefully walking through the courtyard to find many American civilians sleeping on the ground.

This one man walks up to me and places his hand on his lips gesturing me to stay silent. "Are you the Shadow Venom?" he asks in a quiet voice. He looks hopeful, I can't tell why he would be. So, I guess I better find out.

"Whose asking?" I ask, curiously.

He puckers his lips, before releasing with a large smile. "A fellow resister of the Russian attacks," he declared. "We were captured when the Russians were sweeping the area. They took our weapons. We have no way of escaping or fighting back, but we can listen in on the Russian conversation because a few of our guys know Russian. We overheard them tell each other stories about you," I didn't think that anyone else would hear about me, but I guess I'm going to have to live with the fact that people back home may discover my identity, though it's a thought that I fear.

Jeremiah Anderson

"Well, how do we get you guys out?" I ask ready for action.

"Do your thing," he says with a smile, I return it though he cannot see it. I watch as a guard makes his rounds around the fence, he doesn't look too hard to fight. I wait until I see no other guards in the vicinity. Once he renders alone, I take my knife and stab into his neck through the fence before snatching his gun and handing it over to the man. He happily accepts the weapon. "Thank you, my name's Alex," he gives a slight wink of his eye before walking away and removing a brick from the wall. He pulls out a few knives, handing them to some other men who appear out of nowhere. We sneak over to the gate hoping to not draw too much attention to us. I pulled out one of my grenades and released the pin. Throwing the grenade into the gate not only destroys the gate but also causes the fence around it to disappear like it never existed.

I grab my shield and pull out one of my guns, with the help of Alex we storm the place taking out the area of Russians before their minds can even process what is happening. Hate to admit it but I'm beginning to like this Alex guy, he is smart and doesn't act unless prepared, and best of all likes me. Once all the guards have been cleared, we circle back around to the gate, once we meet up Alex thanks everyone for their outstanding job in fighting the

Shadow Venom

Russian troops. Alex reaches out to give me a handshake and I willingly accept it, but something instantly feels wrong. Alex freezes in place with his eyes wide open locked on me. He coughs up blood splattering it all over me before falling to the ground dead. Once he had fallen, I noticed a Russian holding up a gun. I almost have a tear come to my eye, but before releasing it, I walk over to the Russian and stab my knife into his appendix, causing him excruciating pain.

I lead the group of civilians through the forest heading back to town with the help of the armed civilians at my side. Clenching my fists so hard it causes me to lose circulation in my hand for a couple of minutes, but I don't care now. Once we make it out of the forest, we split off in our separate ways and they head off to their families as I head off to retrieve my motorcycle before heading home.

~

Once I reach home, I slip a robe on removing my mask to conceal any hint of me having my suit on in case my mother has received word of the "Shadow Venom." I climb the tree outside the house and easily jump through the window. I turn on the light only to discover my mother sitting on my bed.

Jeremiah Anderson

Before I can say anything, she holds her palm towards me, showing that she needs no explanation. "I know where you have been," She states. Has she discovered what I've been doing? I figured she might discover the Shadow Venom but not that I'm him.

I try to act sincere. "I'm sorry," I say tenderheartedly. Hoping she will forgive me.

"I understand since your father has died..." More like murder, but I understand her point. "... things will be changing. I don't want you to get used to sneaking out too much and doing this. I'm fine with you going out and partying just don't do anything stupid okay?" Partying? Is that what she thinks I'm doing? I nod contently before she suspects anything more. She leans in to kiss me on the cheek before heading off to bed. I fall back on my bed with relief and try to relax before going to bed, hoping that she will never discover what I've been doing.

The next morning, I discovered the school was canceled and would not continue for the rest of the year while the Russian attack was taking place. I find the television already set to the news before grabbing a banana and some orange juice and sitting down. I've thought a lot about Alex since his death and thought about how nice it was to have a partner and I've considered the people that I know who might make both a good partner and have reason to get revenge, but also defend themselves in a fight, and the only person I could think of was Ben.

I hop on my motorcycle and head off to his house. When I reached it I both knocked and rang the doorbell but there was no answer. The entire time that I've known Ben, he has always been here to answer the door. When we were younger, if he went on vacation I was always first to know and when he leaves, he always tells me. I'm always the first to know. I wonder if his family is grieving so much from the death of his father that he just didn't think about it. Come to think of it I haven't reached out to him in days either. Regardless I head home and decide to get some sleep since I won't be very deadly if I'm tired. This is one job you don't want to be asleep on the job for.

I wake up sometime around ten at night. My mother sleeps softly in her room, with a stir in her slumber. I walk downstair and discover the television on with the news playing, showing a helicopter flying over at least seven different Russian bases. I run upstairs quietly and on a piece of paper write this.

Jeremiah Anderson

Dear Mother,

I will be going on a camping trip with one of my friends for a couple of days, I will be back soon.

Love your son.

Hunter.

Quietly packing my bag with my different pieces of gear, I rush out the window into the night.

~

I rode my motorcycle to the forest but decided to continue riding it through the forest this time. It does fine, I only need to be careful that I don't fall into something that would make it difficult to pull a motorcycle out of. Once I reach a long ditch in the ground, I hide my motorcycle in a bush and continue walking. I begin to get hungry, so I look around for a squirrel or a rabbit. As I'm walking, I hear a rabbit jump onto a branch snapping it alerting me of its presence. I turn on my thermal goggles to gain a better idea of where it is. I pull out my dagger and throw it into the rabbit's skull.

Needing someplace to cook it, I start a fire with my flame emitter and cook the rabbit on a stick. Once I'm done eating, I grab some berries to stick in my pocket and continue hiking.

Once I see a campfire from one of the Russian soldier bases, I prepare for the battle ahead. When two of the three soldiers aren't looking, I grab one of the soldiers by the neck, slash his throat with my knife, and drag him into the forest to act as though he was never there. I use my shield and throw it at a soldier's face, not to harm him but to use it as a distraction. I leap up onto the man and kick him to the ground landing my foot on his throat to suffocate him. I grab my shield and arm myself with it once again, blocking the other soldiers' bullets from killing me. I lift my leg to grab my dagger. Jumping up into the air, I stabbed my knife through the soldier's eye socket into his brain. I stab the soldier on the ground in the side with my claws and watch as he bleeds out to death.

I continue to the next campfire and rush in with my katana in one hand and my shield in the other. I slit the throat of one soldier with my katana and sliced the head clean off another. But before I have any time to react the Russian soldier kicks my left lower leg causing me to fall on one knee, he gives a clean kick to my jaw making me fly onto my back. Before he can kill me, I turn on my flame emitter and aim it carefully at his face to blind him and roast him. But he doesn't die quickly or quietly. Forcing me to get up and stab him in the back with my katana finishing the kill.

On the final campfire, I don't feel like messing around too much so I pull out my gun and waste two precious bullets shooting two soldiers in the forehead, both from different spots around the campfire. On the final soldier I choose to keep him, but not unharmed. I aim my gun at his thigh, crouching on one knee. Just as I'm about to pull the trigger, seconds before it makes an impact with the ground a grenade flies next to me yards away, landing in a hole causing the grenade to blow up and sending me flying away into the ground on my arm. My arm feels as though it is broken, though I know it is not.

I lift myself from the ground checking my surroundings to see if there are any soldiers nearby. I arm myself with my shield and claws. I turn around to notice two soldiers running towards me, but before they can lay a finger on me, I release my flame emitter upon them setting them aflame then pulling out my dagger and tripping a soldier causing him to fall onto my dagger, puncturing it through his chest. The other soldier gets roasted to death. Another soldier runs along the top of the concrete wall of the base and attempts to shoot me with his gun. He soon realizes he won't kill me that way, so he unlatches a grenade from his belt pulling out the pin. Before he could throw it. I fired my gun into his skull knocking both him and the grenade back into the base blowing up the place.

I run with all my might trying to get out of range of the explosion before I die a fiery death. Once the explosion ends, I sneak back to gather grenades and bullets I can use later, if they haven't been destroyed yet. Since I have many more days to go until this is done

Chapter 4

I spent the last few nights blowing up bases, and in the day sleeping or getting myself some food. After getting a decent night's sleep in a tree, I retrace all my steps through each of my previously blown-up bases and collect any resources that I can use along the way, such as food.

Upon coming across the base that I blew up a few nights ago, I found the man that I was trying to take alive, lying on the ground behind a bush, with a bandage wrapped around his thigh. I must have shot him and not known it, and after being shot he tried to heal himself. I grabbed hold of his collar and dragged him through the forest until I dragged him back to my motorcycle. I strap him on and push the motorcycle through the forest, until reaching the bridge where I toss him off the ledge into the river, but not before stabbing my claws into his sides causing him to bleed out before he even touches the water.

Shadow Venom

I ride for a half hour or so before pulling over to the side of the road near an old, abandoned warehouse. I change inside of a shed that looks to be falling apart from the inside out. When I'm about to hop back on my motorcycle and head home, I get a strange feeling and look up. It's faint but I can see a man walking away from the window, who which must have seen me. I try to ignore it, regardless of consequences, whoever it is if they pose a threat, I can just kill them.

Once I reached the town, I figured I needed to bring something back for my mother since I left mostly without notice. I didn't know what to bring back, so I stopped by a few veggie stands to make a nice salad when I got back. As I'm about to leave I notice a man having trouble closing the back doors to his large transporting truck. I walk over to offer my help, and without turning around he gladly accepts my offer. I jump onto the truck then grab a grease bottle and pour half the thing on the sides of the door. I grab the rope to the door and jump off the side of the truck to put my full body weight on it, slamming the door shut. The man turns around and I recognize him easily, it's that man I saw the other day who was leading a group of men to fight the Russian bases.

Jeremiah Anderson

He gives me a gentle smile, with a pat on my back. "Well thank you, young man," he pauses for a second. "Do I know you from somewhere?"

I don't need him discovering my little secret identity, so I just try to act as though I've never met him before. "No, I don't believe so. You might be thinking of someone different." He nods contently and continues to finish what he is doing. I try to slip out before he can ask any more questions and figure out who I am.

I make a quick stop by Ben's house to see if he is home, but by looking at his gaming system, I see dust has accumulated on it. Which means he must not have been home for a couple of days. For as long as I can remember he has never really gone more than two days without playing games, even when his father would ground him. Despite Mr. Damien being a killer, he is quite soft and often lets Ben play even then. If there's nothing else for me to do, then I figure the best thing for me to do is head home.

Once I'm back I park my motorcycle in the usual spot and head for the front door. I quickly throw my bag into the bush out front, so my mother doesn't assume it to be dirty laundry and try to take it from me. I open the door carelessly to alert my mother of my presence, but upon turning on the light, I discover drops of blood along the ground. I rush outside to grab both my knife and shield for protection, then proceed to follow the trail of blood. The blood is fresh. I expect to find my mother somewhere struggling to survive with some Russian soldier over her stabbing her to death. Instead, I find Ben resting on the table with his throat ripped out. I feel a change in the room, my chest hurts like a rhino charged at it at full speed, the same way I felt when my father died. Except this time, I watch as my best friend lays there on the table unable to joke around with me the way he always did. But no, he lies there dead.

I look around and try to focus my eyes on one object. But everything spins around me like I'm trapped in some tornado. My eyes are teary. My fingers are numb. I want to know who did this. I slam my fists onto the table demanding answers. And this is what I'm told.

Ben was sleeping in his room after spending all day playing video games, then suddenly in the night Mrs. Wilde heard Ben's window slap shut, so she rushed upstairs to discover her son in this state, so she waited till morning to bring him over.

I was slightly confused since I was just at his house, and I looked at his gaming system to discover that it was accumulated with dust. Dust doesn't accumulate that fast. But I have no reason to disbelieve it, so I just nod in discomfort. I fight back tears from flowing down my face as I wander into the garage, sitting at my workbench. Wondering what to do next.

I noticed the battery pack I got from school, there is no better motivation for me to complete it than the motivation to get revenge on my new enemy. The project I'm working on is an arm brace much in the same style as my flame emitter, but this one has a metal plate on my fist. When I turn it on theoretically it should have an electric shock on any person or animal it comes in contact with. But it isn't just for shocking the person I want to punch. It's also shocking me. The wires that go along my hand to a metal plate on my fingers are sending shocks into me as well as the person I'm trying to electrocute. I haven't been quite able to put it together just right yet, but it is meant to be an electrified venom punch. It's meant to feel as though someone is getting venom shocked into them. When I'm finished, I should be able to use it in my suit. However, I fear that if I make it too strong. I would shock myself by being close to the enemy. So, it will only be strong enough to put someone out of action for a little while. With the potential to kill them. Though before I use it, it will take some time to find the right amount of shock to put out, so I will set it on a low setting for the time being.

Shadow Venom

I need something to get my mind off the imminent death of my best friend, and I can't think of a better place to go than the place to go and to get my mind off things. My self-defense class.

My teacher Master Kim has been teaching at the studio for ten years and has gotten to know me very well. I started when I was five. He has been teaching me how to defend myself ever since, I've never been in a school fight because I've always been a passive kid, but Ben has always been in school fights for as long as I can remember. And these classes gave him the upper hand in all those fights.

I begin the class with a few minor stretches before exercising different muscle-building techniques. Then I move on to various kicks and punches. At the end of every class, Master Kim picks two students to fight each other. So, they can learn more about a more person style of how to fight that's unique to them, rather than just using what he has taught. I'm chosen to face Gideon Yael, the largest kid in our class. The other students stand in a circle about ten feet away from us to cheer on their choice fighter, the losers must do an extreme workout challenge decided by the winners at the end, like one thousand pushups every day, for a week.

Jeremiah Anderson

Gideon throws a few punches in my direction. I block each one without any effort. Which is strange because I've never been able to do that before. He senses this and throws another quicker punch to my face but as I go to block it, he kicks my lower leg leaving me on one knee.

Suddenly I'm back in the situation I was in days ago. I'm in my suit but with no mask, no weapons, no gloves, nothing to defend myself with. So, I run towards the soldier hoping to survive, I try to block the bullets but almost everyone hits me, feeling more like a punch rather than a bullet. I leap onto the soldier placing my knees on his shoulders and squeezing them around his neck. Punching continuously till he falls on the ground not dead but knocked out.

Bright light comes to my face, I'm back in the studio. When I finally can render my surroundings correctly, I see everyone holding one another scared looking at me like some monster. I look around not sure why. Until I spot Gideon, on the floor with his face bruised and bleeding out of his mouth and nose. His eyes look like they are cracked and broken. He's not dead but certainly in need of medical attention. I ran out of the building before anyone could stop me, and quickly jumped onto my motorcycle and headed home.

Shadow Venom

I lay on my bed for a couple of hours not moving more than I should have to, thinking about what did. After many hours of thinking about what I have become, I decided that it's for the best, it gives me strength to destroy those who have harmed me, and if a few people must get hurt on the way, then so be it. I will avenge my father and Ben. I sneak downstairs to get some food since I haven't had a decent meal in a little while, especially since my father died. I take a few buns and spread some honey on them. I also got some carrots and a few other fruits and veggies to eat.

I hear someone coming around the corner, but the footsteps sound heavier than my mother's. I grab a carrot in my hand, though it isn't that useful as a weapon it is the closest thing to me. The person gets closer to the corner. I leap out in front of them.

It's only my mother. Her eyes are wide open and shocked. "Cool down soldier," she says genuinely concerned. She looks into my eyes and sees genuine fear in them.

"Yes, I'm fine just gave me a scare," I say feeling guilt come upon me.

"I scared you?" she asks. "Well then that evens out the points now, doesn't it?" she says trying to calm me down from stabbing her to death using a carrot.

"Yep, I guess it does," I say shyly. Sliding the carrot behind my back acting as though would make the moment disappear.

She gives me a tight squeeze and then pushes me away gently. "Get to bed, get a good night's sleep, no parties tonight, okay? You need to keep your strength up to go to them." She gives a slight wink to me.

I walk up the stairs with a small smile on my face, but then it hits me. What was that wink for? I wonder to myself. What could it mean? Maybe she was just trying to mess around with me, yeah that's all it can be right?

I lie there for hours on end getting no sleep, fearing what I have become, but reflecting on how I decided it was for the best. I stare out my window watching the sky as the clouds float by in the bright moonlight. Suddenly a figure flies by in front of my window. I jump out of bed fearing for my mother's safety, but I can hear him entering the house through the window in the hall, passing my mother's room, coming for me. I lay back down in bed, trying to act as though I was asleep, I hear the door creak open, it appears to be someone of a similar size but slightly taller than me. I see his shadow reaching over me preparing to kill me.

Without thinking I throw myself out of bed onto this mysterious killer, smashing him into my dresser. I attempt to strangle him with clothing, but before I can suffocate him, he punches me in the gut throwing me into the wall with more force than I had prepared for. He pulls out a katana much like mine. He swings the sword at my face. Aiming for the kill. I bend back before even a single hair is cut. I reach under my bed grab my katana and engage in a deadly sword fight against this monster.

He seems to enjoy going for my head, allowing me to anticipate his attack using it to my advantage, and allowing me to steal the blade from his hand and throw it to the side. For a moment I believe he is weaponless. But he lifts his leg and grabs a dagger from his boot, the same place I store my knives. That's when I noticed it, his suit is exactly like mine! He has every weapon I have. The only difference is, instead of having a plain black suit like mine, his suit is black with white and gold highlights.

He jumps up high to stab me, but I roll under him and swiftly search my desk for my electrified venom shocker. I attach it to my left arm and prepare to punch the life out of him. He leaps in again to stab me but this time I give a punch straight to his chest sending an electric shock through his entire body. Causing him to fly back into the wall. The posters on my wall are torn, and the shelves no longer hold anything. But I'm willing to lose a small cactus's life than my own. I cautiously approached him, trying to not make too much sound to wake him. I stare at him for a few moments, I figure I at least deserve to know the identity of my killer, so I carefully try to pull his mask off. But before I can pull it above his chin, he grabs my leg and yanks it causing me to fall flat on my back. Before I can react, he grabs me by the neck and places his foot on my left arm to prevent me from shocking him again. He lifts and slams me into the wall. In the perfect position to kill me, but I can tell he hesitates.

He stares at me for a few moments before trying to talk. "I tried to save you," he releases me before escaping out my window. I catch my mother standing in the doorway with her hand covering her mouth, scared to the bone.

She bends down to grab my shoulders and look me in the eye. Staring at me like she thought she was going to lose me, which she might have. "Next time you party, don't get hurt."

Shadow Venom

"I…" I freeze before I can say anything else, or even begin to explain.

"No, just do what you must, you're stronger than you have ever realized. And I think you're just figuring that out," I can tell she knows something about what I have been doing. But how much does she know?

She walks away with a few tears in her eyes. I sit on my bed for a few minutes trying to take in what just happened. I don't know who this guy is, but he nearly killed me, I need to make sure that doesn't happen again. There's only one more thing I can do, and that's to finish my electrified venom shocker. I spend hours upon hours working on it trying to get it just right because I would like to try and kill the enemy with a single punch.

But I also don't want him to kill me.

Chapter 5

After spending so much time working on the gear. I take a break to watch the news. Even after fighting me last night, the monster killed my neighbor in his sleep by tearing out his throat. I don't know what I'm going to do about this. First, my father dies then my best friend. I can't even believe this. I try to come up with my next plan of action, starting with the main thing, and that's to find this guy and kill him. If he truly is the one who killed my best friend, then he's the one I want dead. I can't help but wonder if this is connected to the Russian infiltration. I plan to find him tonight but first. I need to learn as much about this guy before I take him out. So far, I know he mainly kills his victims by ripping their throats out, he also has every weapon I have, except my electrified venom shocker. I will use that knowledge to my advantage, if I assume that he thinks somewhat like me that could give me a clue as to what he might do next, and that's continue what he started.

Shadow Venom

Night has fallen, and my mother is asleep, so I've climbed onto my roof and waited silently in my full suit ready to face him. I listen to the different sounds of the night, crickets chirping, trees swaying and owls hooting. Off in the distance I hear the faint scream of a woman, I notice a figure jumping from the roof of a building. I slide down the side of my house and onto the ground. I chase after the figure. He must be the guy that attacked me the other night. I catch him climbing a very large building, he makes it to the top before I begin climbing.

When I reach the roof, I don't see him anywhere. It's as if he vanished, I check behind a few boxes and other things before giving up. I get ready to run and jump off the roof when I get shoved to the ground, completely unprepared for it. I roll over on my back and there he is. Standing there is the guy who wants me dead. He pulls out his katana and tries to chop my head off again. I pull out mine as well and block his attacks not attempting to go for him because I wish to study his fighting style. He puts his katana away, realizing he won't get a single drop of blood on me.

Reaching down he chooses to use daggers. He charges at me with all his speed. I grab mine only to match him as we fight. Possibly to death. He gives many good swings at me trying to go for pretty much any exposed part of my body. However, I expected that and made sure to be extra cautious. He winds up giving up and tries to pull out his gun on me. I go for my shield first for protection, then go for my gun to get back on a more offensive side. We fire our guns at each other's heads but both of us block using our shields. I aim for his legs to take him out, but he has some sort of armor on them, so I can't fire there. He attempts the same on me but suspecting he might try it I crouch down and use the shield to block my whole body. Taking advantage of this he runs towards me putting full force of a kick into the shield knocking me over.

With me in such a vulnerable state, he tries to use his flame emitter to force me into defeat. But before it can harm me, I place my shield in front in defense, blocking any chance he has of roasting me. I can tell he is getting better, as though failing is helping him. Is that all he has been doing? Learning my fighting style? He's been trying to study me as I have been him. I threw my shield at him to hit him in the face and block him from seeing me. I grabbed hold of his neck putting him in a position almost impossible to escape alive. I slam him against a shed on the roof making it difficult to escape.

Shadow Venom

My claws are around his neck and at any moment I can finish this. "This is over, you won't be trying to kill me or anyone else again." I tightened my grip before letting my claws slide around his neck. I expect to see him bleeding out. But he's not. He stands there perfectly fine, other than a cut on his mask. I looked through the cut, to find that he had some metal guarding around it. He must have known from my past victims at the bases.

He suddenly throws his dagger at my arm just barely missing it leaving a small cut, distracting me for a few moments. Then leaping onto me putting me on the ground. He holds another dagger above my head ready to send it straight through my skull. With almost sheer instinct I reach my arm over to turn on my electrified venom shocker, then send a punch into his chest, making him fly back into a wall. He must have found a way to block out some of the shock, allowing it to not instantly kill him. He stands up with almost ease. Before preparing to continue fighting.

This monster, I must know more about him. I suppose there's only one way to find out. "Who are you?" I try to stall as much as I possibly can before I can find a way to kill him.

Jeremiah Anderson

He almost growls at me replying. "The Dark Condemner," he picks up a grenade pulling the pin and throwing it in my direction. I roll over as fast as possible getting maybe thirteen feet away before feeling it push me nearly completely off the roof. I dangle for dear life, using all my strength to hold on. Once I pull myself up, I find The Dark Condemner gone.

~

The next morning, I woke up and as usual, I watched the news and ended up seeing my whole fight broadcasted on television. At the end of the news story about me and The Dark Condemner, there is an announcement that there will be school today but starting at ten in the morning, so I get dressed for school since I still would like an education almost as much taking out the evil Russians.

I rode my motorcycle up to school wearing a nice black shirt and a pair of blue pants. I pull into the parking lot and as usual, I watch Chloe walking into school looking as beautiful as ever. Taking me by surprise the school news anthem plays giving the announcements. I exhaled in relief, fearing that was the sound of a Russian bugle taking over the school. I ignore the announcements for the most part until I hear that they are having a school dance. I know who I want to ask but at the same time, I wonder if it's a good idea. I mean my life is in consistent danger right now and the last people I want to harm are the people I care about. Well, what's left of those people?

I go through school the whole day wondering how I will ask Chloe to the school dance. I could get a bunch of people in on it and throw a big surprise or I can do something small. I decided to ask casually as friends, but we both knew we would act like more than friends at the dance.

I walk up to her acting so above everyone else and giving her a nice smile. "Hey, girl, nice shoes. So, how about going with me to that dance? As friends?" I ask her nicely, almost smugly. In a way, she can't refuse.

"Um… No, I don't want to go to the dance with you…" my heart sinks almost as though another person I care about has just died. She has never said no to me before. Was it Ben that she liked all this time, and she was only using me to make him jealous? A smile begins to grow on her face. "… As friends," she says leaning in and giving a small kiss on my cheek, with a wink. My cheeks turning red with embarrassment, I lean back in to return the kiss, then head off.

Jeremiah Anderson

"Wear something pretty!" I yell, though that girl could wear rags and she would still be the prettiest girl I've ever met. She smiles and then gets back to talking to her friends. I headed back home with a smile on my face. I know that almost no bad thing could take that away from me. I plop down on my couch to get some rest after this long and exhausting day.

I wake up the next day at seven in the morning, to find out that today is the day of Ben's funeral. I dressed myself in complete black wearing a nice suit I was planning on wearing for the school dance, but I decided this was my best friend's funeral. I might as well show a little respect rather than showing up in sweat clothes. My mother comes into my room and sits on my bed to tell me how this is going to be hard, and that it's okay to think about him from time to time. I know everything she says to be true I have given the same speech to others before. But I know my mother is only trying to comfort me on this day.

I continued to get dressed until I found the watch Ben stole when we were younger. We were both getting ready for the fourth grade when I got really scared and I ran away from the building when I was dropped off, but Ben being the crazy dude he is, made an offer that still appalls me to this day. He said that if I went to school, he would steal something expensive for me from anyone I wanted. I agreed to his deal. So, I went on to school and had fun, well about as much fun as you can at school in the fourth grade. And at the end of the day, it was time for me to tell him who I wanted him to steal something from. I decided I wanted Ben to steal from Dmitry Slovak. A Russian criminal was caught in an alley killing two teenagers for their food. I was mortified by him, which is why I thought Ben would back down to steal his watch. But no, Ben did not. The next day He shows up to school wearing the watch around his wrist with the smuggest look I had ever seen, along with a matching scar over his left eye, which has faded over the years but is still present.

I fall to my knees just thinking about Dmitry, fearing that something bad will happen to my mother like a bomb goes off and losing one of the last people that I truly care about. I still have tears in my eyes, but I pull myself together long enough to make it to the car.

No! I shouldn't be this crushed. I'm a ruthless killer now. I need to toughen up and fight this masked killer. The Dark Condemner. I'm sure that Ben would want me to go on and avenge those that I care about. I must stay strong; I can give in to this pain I feel. But if I can hide it maybe I can control it, use it to my advantage.

We arrive at the graveyard where the funeral is being held for Ben. My mother considered holding a funeral for my father, but we decided to hold off till after the Russian invasion. But I wonder why Mrs. Wilde didn't wait as well. The ceremony starts slowly. Mostly because Mrs. Wilde was crying the whole time through it, she talks about how much Ben loved to hang out with me, and all those sorts of things. I take a good look around and notice none of Ben's other friends are here. That does make me slightly suspicious because even though I'm his best friend, surely his other friends would show up. As I watch a group of men carry his body down the aisle it almost feels like he's on the other side of a barrier even I cannot access, even if I died a thousand deaths. He was such a good person I don't even think he would consider fighting alongside me. He's always been a tough guy and got into fights a lot, but I'm not so sure he would ever kill anyone. But he was always there for me. I have a debt to him I can never repay.

They open the casket, and he just lies there, still, and breathless. I mean that's kind of what a dead body does anyway. I don't know what else I expected, a choreographed musical number of him dancing into his grave. I finally give away at my tough guy act and kneel at the casket and cry. It takes every ounce of will in my body to not steal his body and try to bring it back to life.

Once my throat clears, I stand up accepting my best friend's fate, and try to move on. I got to head back to my seat, but something caught my eye. Someone is watching from on top of a distant building. I try to focus my eyes on this figure, then once I get a closer look, I realize it's The Dark Condemner. How sicker can he get? He comes to watch the funeral of his victims, and afterward is he going to continue to slaughter children, helpless innocent children? I know he is looking at me, but why? Is it because I defeated him when he tried to kill me? But what was he trying to say when he told me "I tried to save you." I may never know.

The service ends and people are released to do what they wish. I usually go running with Ben, but I don't think Ben will be able to do that given his circumstances. So, I decided to walk over to the group of neighborhood mothers that my mom seemed too keen to hang out with. They stand there in a circle crying, endlessly. I didn't know they liked Ben that much. Most mothers in the neighborhood despised his family because of what his father used to do. My father knew Mr. Damien wanted to do what was best for his family, so my father helped him get a good restart in life.

After listening to them for a couple of minutes, I found out that they were crying because all of them had lost a son to The Dark Condemner in the night. I didn't realize how many people lost someone to this guy. But the last few nights have been "better," no one has had as much of a problem with him. I now know there is more to avenge than the death of my father, than the death of Ben. I need to avenge the death of every man and woman who lost their life during the attack of this Russian invasion. My first target will be The Dark Condemner.

Only this time, I'm not going to let him escape alive. I don't even want one drop of his blood to be left.

I will not rest until every Russian terrorist's blood has been eliminated.

Vengeance will be mine.

<u>Chapter 6</u>

After spending all night working on a plan to defeat The Dark Condemner, I think I just might have the perfect plan. It should be inescapable, and impossible for him to win at. I did consider grouping those guys who were taking off the Russian bases, but I want to take his life personally. I ended up spending a couple of hours at my local hardware store because, for my plan to work, I would need some supplies. Plus, the store owner will refuse to tell anyone who has or hasn't bought something from the store, so I won't have to worry about the word getting out that I bought all this stuff. I grab a few large nets with some flame-resistant sprays to go with them. I don't want his death to be quick. He will not have the chance to run.

Next, I head over to the store next door and grab a few smoke machines, after that, I pack everything in my bag and head to my next destination. My plan involves my town's relaxation garden building. The building is circular with a hole in the middle, with a paved path surrounded by beautiful exotic flowers. It won't be beautiful much longer. The roof slants down to the inside of the circle, it will make the perfect trap for The Dark Condemner.

Finally, I head to every house that has lost a child to The Dark Condemner. It was for the most part, easy, though these guys were my friends. The interviews don't usually take that long, I basically must see how many questions I can ask before they start crying all over again.

Except one. Mrs. Lyman's son Peter. She almost completely accepts what happened. She doesn't seem to mind it very much. She sits me down on her couch and immediately tells me this story.

Mrs. Lyman was going upstairs to check on Peter because she thought he was up using some of his electrical equipment again. His father is an electrician, so he is interested in electrical stuff as well, and seldom puts it down. When she opens the door, she sees some figure in a mostly black suit with gold and white highlights. I already knew that he killed her son, but she just makes the story so exhilarating. She proceeds to tell me how she caught him going through her son's box of electrical stuff. As The Dark Condemner is reading a book, he gets caught off guard to find Mrs. Lyman watching him go through Peter's stuff. So, The Dark Condemner turns around to Peter and slashes him in the throat before jumping out of the window.

She begins to cry so I take that as my signal to leave. Though right as I'm about to. I spotted some electrical books on the floor next to some of Peter's things. I pick it up and it says, "How electricity impacts the human body." The Dark Condemner must have been trying to figure out how I was able to gain such strength using my electrified venom shocker. After discovering this I figure I've gotten everything that I need, he's certainly fascinated by what I can do. I hop back on my motorcycle. As usual, it gives me trouble. But I managed to get it started back up again. On the way back, I discover some mysterious group of men sneaking into the woods. They look to be wearing some sort of strong military uniform. It's unique, it's completely black with a helmet that has a mouth guard and a clear glass to see out of. They also have this symbol on their back that appears to be the mixture of a snake, spider, and wasp. I became overly curious as to what they were. I am considering following them. But I won't fight well in the daylight. So, I continued back home.

Jeremiah Anderson

I spend a little while watching the news and get a little more familiar with where the bases are so I can be more efficient in getting rid of them. After I'm finished I clean, and ready my weapons to fight The Dark Condemner. After I'm done, I head to bed to dream about every possible way I can kill The Dark Condemner to get revenge on him for what he has taken from me.

~

It's the middle of the night when I wake up. I spend a few minutes trying to think of any holes in my plan, and one that I never considered before comes up. What if he kills me? If he were to win, he could escape and kill more people, that's why I need to make sure I don't die. Or if I do I need to make sure we both go down. Maybe I should get some backup. In case something does happen.

I search my pockets for the card from the leader of the rebellion. It has an address written on it. It looks like the address of an old warehouse in the industrial part of town. After changing into my suit, I got on my motorcycle to ride off to the warehouse. When I reach the industrial buildings, they look as they always do. Broken and torn down, like some sort of horror ghost town. When I was younger, I used to explore this place with my father. In the daylight, when it felt safer.

Shadow Venom

When I located the building. I give numerous strong kicks to get the door open, but it still won't budge. I take a few steps back from the door and use all my power to run into the door and extend my leg to kick it open. I look around for signs of these fighters, but I see nothing. I spent a few more minutes looking but I finally gave up. I remember something. I recall that there was a giant furnace. Behind it was this giant room. I never knew what it was used for, but I do know that it's where I would hide. When I find the furnace, I crawl through it to a large vent in the back, until it gets larger and larger as I go down it. I try to stay on track by placing my hand on the wall and walking down through the hall till I find a light shining brightly through a door creaking open. I sneak up to it peeking through the crack, I can see the leader of the rebellion, along with a bunch of other people standing in the long halls surrounding him.

I lean in closer to get a better look, but I lose my footing and fall forward into the room. I catch myself before I can hit the ground, and immediately stand back up. Numerous men aim their guns at me ready to shoot me before I can even blink.

Jeremiah Anderson

Their leader signals them to put down their guns. Showing how he approves of my little visit. "Why hello, I didn't know you would be joining us."

I decided to act a little above them all, in the hope of giving me a decent stature. "Well, I figured it was about time, plus I need a favor," I point out. He nods willingly to hear me out. "I plan to take out The Dark Condemner. Ever heard of him? He kills children in their sleep." I know that I'm being a little insensitive, but what does it matter?

He looks at me disapproving of my choice of wording. "Vaguely, but I don't know too much about him. What do you need me for?"

"I require some backup, I prefer to handle most of this myself, I have some personal business. I will signal when and if I need help." I don't need them to do all my work for me. I want to make sure he feels the pain and anguish that I feel. Every. Single. Day. Because of people like him.

He looks at me unsure of what I ask, but he chooses to proceed anyway. "What would be the signal?"

"Me drawing my last breath," I stared at him into his eyes trying to figure out whether he takes me seriously or not. "So will you help me or not?" He starts with a serious, stern look in his eyes. But drifts into a smile. I tap my foot showing my impatience.

"Take a look at this," he presses a button under the table turning on a light, showcasing a bunch of suits. The same suits I saw on a couple of men the other day. "These suits were made after your own, I've seen how much effort and focus you have put into this thing, and I've decided that I want you to help us take this thing down."

"Why?" I wonder why someone would want to have me on their team. I'm not the sort of person who works well with large groups of people.

"Many see you as a hero. You have single-handedly taken down so many bases alone. We've noticed the amount of skill you have, and I figured maybe one day you would need us like we need you to win this thing. So, we figured we would back you up, and you can back us up," he says with passion and focus, as though he had been standing in the bathroom for hours practicing.

"Um… I don't know what to say." I'm genuinely unsure, because if I accept it then I'm forced to worry about the safety of others. If I turn it down. I went through all this trouble for nothing.

"Say nothing, just accept it. We call them the Strike Back Stingers, we don't know which venom-related animal you were going for, so we chose wasps."

I stared blankly at him for a few moments to make my decision. "Thank you." I didn't consider the impact that I would be having on others. It's affecting everyone, not just the enemy.

"Hey, even the smallest actions can have the largest impacts. Oh, I never told you, my name. I'm Mark." He must have figured out my secret identity. At least I believe that I can trust him, though it feels a little weird that he randomly tells me his name. I do feel slightly suspicious about that.

After I wrap things up, I hop back on my motorcycle and head to the relaxation gardens. My plan is complete the time has come. I sit on the roof waiting patiently for my foe to arrive. The moment I see him, and he lands on this roof, I plan to push him into the pit. I will then drop the nets down the sides of the inside of the building then set them aflame to trap us inside. And to make it more difficult I will have the fog machine, along with glass sculptures to block his thermal goggles. And in the situation that I die, the Strike Back Stingers will shoot him through a few windows inside the building. The end goal, he dies.

Shadow Venom

I spend maybe twenty minutes setting the trap and instructing the Strike Back Stingers to their places. The Dark Condemner doesn't show up the first night, or the second or the third. Finally, on the fourth, I get there a little early seeing as I figure he might get here earlier than I thought as well.

Sitting there relaxed and ready to fight this guy and get it over with, I become a little nervous. Because if I die there will be no one else left to take care of my mother. But I must win, because I'm given a fighting chance. Ben was not. I hear a faint scream off in the distance, he must be close, I can see him running on the roofs of buildings not far away, it's not till I see him, and he sees me that I feel a few chills. He leaps off the building disappearing into the night. But I stand guard just in case. When I'm about to leave I hear the faint sound of panting right behind me.

We stand still refusing to make the first move, both silent and unsure. I choose to break the silence. "Have you come to kill me?" I ask rhetorically.

"Only if you think you deserve it," I almost take offense to that comment since I'm not the one who murdered innocent children in their sleep. I murdered evil Russian soldiers, who were at least awake. Now he's getting on my nerves.

Jeremiah Anderson

I might be able to get out some useful information before I kill him. "So, why me? Why do you come after me?"

"Simple, you're the biggest threat to the Russians. You've been taking out too many bases." I was right, he is not only connected to the Russian terrorist attack, but he's part of it.

"So, I'm punished for doing my job?"

"All you need to know is that there will be peace when you are dead."

"Peace huh?" He stands there motionless, barely even moving his chest to breathe. Not even making the slightest sound.

"Well let's get this started, shall we?" I give him a simple nod, stepping back into a fighting stance. He chooses to use his shield and dagger. I switch on my electrified venom shocker. He leaps up with his arms over his head attempting to stab me. I slide underneath, careful not to fall from the roof. I reach for his leg, grabbing it with all my strength and using it as leverage to throw him back to the metal plating that is the roof. Before he can notice me, I slide under him and use my electrified venom shocker to blast him into the garden.

Shadow Venom

He flies off the roof landing in a small pond within the gardens. He looks conscious but dazed. I quickly release the nets and set them on fire using my flame emitter before he regains consciousness. I set the smoke machines in the garden previously. The ground is now covered in a thick fog. He tries to shoot me aimlessly shooting in every direction.

I jump from the roof into the garden hiding in the bushes, concealing myself from his line of sight. I rolled behind him and put him in a chokehold. And to finish my attack I sweep his feet to the ground before he can gain any sort of leverage against me.

"Ready for this to end," I say threateningly towards him.

"Not just yet," he uses his claws to slash my arm, forcing me to release him from my grip. He swings his body around and lands a kick into my face. Throwing me on my side. I stand back up brushing off the kick quickly, knowing that if I do not, I will die. I try to look for him, but he's nowhere to be seen. That's when I realized, my weapon had become his weapon too. He sweeps my feet, making me land on my back. He holds his katana to my neck, ready to stab through. I grab hold of it, with it between my two palms. I quickly point it in another direction and use this chance to kick him off balance. He stumbles onto his back into the pond. I jump onto him and with both hands, I hold his head under the water trying to drown him.

He moves quickly and reaches for my mask trying to slip it off. I quickly grabbed his wrists, twisted them, and locked him into a painful pressure point. He kicks me in the stomach pushing me back. Before I can get back up, he climbs out of the water jittering with anger. Or maybe it's cold? He pulled out his gun trying to fire at me, but I was one step ahead and had my shield ready. I throw my shield at his face, but he just ducks and shoots me inside of my calf. He doesn't hesitate to try and roast me with his flame emitter. I duck around the foliage as a cover till I retrieve my shield and block his flames from reaching me.

My shield blocks the flame as well as my view, and he knows that. After a few moments of peace, my shield is pulled away from me. I got punched in the face and stomach. I try to go in for a punch myself, but it is dodged easily. He grabs me by the shoulder, pulls me in to give me another punch to the gut, and pushes me away to the ground while pulling my mask off. Revealing my identity. He stands there almost shocked to finally see who I am. The mask was getting stuffy anyway and he will die tonight so it won't matter.

Shadow Venom

I used my electrified venom shocker to punch him in the chest, blasting him through the door of the building. He lies on the ground anxious, but I can't tell what about. I unclip the grenade from my belt pull the pin from it, and instinctively throw it to the ceiling above him. It blows up the entire half of the building, it throws me back into the wall on the other side of the garden. The nets of fire come down blowing in the wind, the building soon goes up in smoke. I can hear sirens wailing as the building catches fire and burns to the ground.

I can finally feel the bullet in my leg as I try to walk away. As well as the I the stick logged in my ribs. Not far enough in to kill me but enough to cause pain. My mind is more rested than it has been in a little while, the Dark Condemner is dead, and I have avenged Ben. But things will not be made right until every Russian terrorist's blood is dripping from my blade.

Part 2

"The bloodshed."

Chapter 7

I have gotten some better sleep the last few nights since the banishment of The Dark Condemner. Before I can get a few hours of relaxation I get a call from Chloe asking me to come over to discuss what dress she should wear. I don't care but I know she wears, but any excuse to hang out with Chloe is a great one.

She lives at the edge of the neighborhood whereas I live in the dead center. I knock on her door patiently waiting for someone to answer. As the door opens joy jumps through my bones, but it quickly fades when I see her father standing there half naked.

"Who are you? I don't care. Go away," he says angrily. Trying to get rid of me. I walk away to head home, but I hear Chloe call my name softly from the window on the second floor. I climb up the tree right outside her window, and then I latch onto the windowsill and jump in.

She greets me with a big hug. "I hope you didn't have too much trouble with my dad," Chloe says. Her father doesn't like Ben and me. He doesn't like Ben for the same reason most people don't. Because his father was a vicious killer. And he doesn't like me because I'm friends with the son of a vicious killer. Honestly, I think he hates most people. It's probably the only thing that keeps him sane, like how I imagine me shoving my dagger into the skull of whoever decided to kill my father.

I don't want to be rude, so I'll play along. "No not at all," I say sarcastically. She just smiles and lays some dresses on her bed and goes on to explain why she likes each one.

"So, I want to match you, what will you be wearing?" She asks, but I haven't thought about it. I honestly haven't cared too much either.

"Did you see what I wore at Ben's funeral? I will be wearing that," I say with a goofy crooked smile.

She glares at me as her jaw drops. "Why would you want to wear that? All it's going to do is remind you of Ben. You know he was my best friend too."

Shadow Venom

"Yeah, well what's wrong with thinking about Ben during the dance?" I suppose she does have a point. I will feel only that more depressed about him by thinking about him. I don't need to be sobbing during the slow dance.

"That's why. You're feeling too depressed. I intend to turn that around. I want you to make you, your old happy self again," she pulls out this picture of a suit with vibrant colors that are so bright they could blind a man.

I almost tremble in fear from looking at the suit. "Um no," I say with my eyes wide open. She begs me to wear the suit, but I continuously refuse because I just know that even the nerds would beat me up if I wore that. "Okay compromise, I'll wear the tie, and I'll wear a nice white shirt, but I get my midnight black suit, deal?" She agrees to the compromise almost instantly. Almost as though it's what she wanted all along.

I climbed out of her window back into the tree. Throwing myself from the tree. I landed on the ground.

The walk home is nice with the sunlight on my face and body, with the breeze riding through my hair. I soak as much in as possible because I head back to the bases tonight. When I reached home, I remember I never thanked

Jeremiah Anderson

Mark for helping me fight The Dark Condemner. I plan to thank him later tonight, so in the meantime, I will try to relax as much as possible, since I need to keep my energy up to fight those bases.

~

Sleeping for only a couple of hours. Dusk approaches. I put on my suit before heading back to the warehouse to thank Mark. I ride my motorcycle out there, but I'm running low on fuel. So, I made a quick stop at the gas station to fill up. While I stand there, I see a man dressed in black sneak into the store. I watch curiously as the man points his gun at the store employee. I look closer and see that it's Mrs. Wilde. Ben's mom. I'm quick to run over and hide behind some shelves.

He has a deep voice. That makes him sound bigger than he is. "I don't want any trouble, ma'am, just hand over the money," he says nudging the gun against the thin piece of plastic that separates him from Mrs. Wilde.

"I'm sorry. I can't do that," she says clearly in fear but refusing to give up money that isn't her own. Why won't she hand him the money? It will keep her from being killed.

Shadow Venom

I take a can and throw it into the wall at the other end of the room, causing him to draw his attention to it. I sneak around the counter to find Mrs. Wilde behind it. I can see his shadow moving closer, I turn on my electrified venom shocker, to make this quick.

He notices that Mrs. Wilde has disappeared, so he steps around the side of the counter. As he comes around the corner, I punch him, sending him flying back into the wall at the other side of the store. I'm quick to run over and to hold his neck in my hands.

"So, you think it's fun to play with other people's lives huh? Well, let's see how you like it." I squeeze his throat tighter and tighter in my hand.

"No, please. I can't bear violence. Just turn him into the police. There is no need for murder," she cries, even mourning for the man. I can't tell why. After everything that's happened to her. I don't think she can watch much more of it.

Anger gets the best of me, and I grab my dagger and stab it into his heart. I twist it before pulling it out. She bursts into tears, but I almost don't mind since she almost died. I ran for my motorcycle and got on it before the cops could come.

As I pull in next to the warehouse, I think back to what Mrs. Wilde said. She didn't want me to hurt the man even though it wouldn't have affected her. Jumping off the motorcycle I noticed the door to the warehouse was blocked. I will need another way to get in. I figure if I can do it why not waste my talent? I climb up a sturdy gutter to the next window above. The floor on the second level has been demolished, so I use the vines along the wall to climb down. When I finish, I look around and find that they have not only moved upstairs, but they have at least two hundred people taking refuge.

"Well, if it isn't our local hero. The Shadow Venom." Mark approached me, seemingly knowing what I'd come for. It's like he knows everything, I'm surprised he wasn't able to prevent this thing from happening in the first place.

"There is no need to thank me, I'm just doing my job," he gives a bright smile of appreciation then turns around to give me a quick tour of their new base of operations. This is what he told me.

Shadow Venom

They moved upstairs because if this place were to get bombed then it would crumble on them anyway. So, if they bunk upstairs, they can escape more easily. Plus, they would be completely helpless in that furnace vent, leaving them at the mercy of the Russians.

I show my gratitude for the tour and leave as quickly as I can. I prepare to head off to the forest to defeat more bases, but right as I'm about to leave I hear footsteps from behind me.

"Hey, before you leave, I just wanted to say I would be thrilled if you decided to work with us, as a team. Like all the time not just one single night," I consider the offer, but I just don't think that I should. Because I don't want to look out for others as well as myself. Plus, I teamed with them once, and working together constantly would be tiring since I don't already have a partner. Well, I did. But he's dead.

"Thank you for the offer but I will work alone for the time being." I excuse myself from the situation and ride off towards the forest. When I reach the edge of the forest, I hide my motorcycle near the water behind a bush. I shouldn't be too long so I shouldn't have to worry about water rising and getting the motorcycle wet. The bridge below me is an old concrete piece of junk. I wouldn't trust it to hold a leaf.

I hike through the forest along tall skinny trees that don't provide much cover, but they lead me to this road. It's the road that the Russians have been using to transport their goods. I walk alongside it, though it's dangerous because they could shoot me from behind before I can tell that they are there. For the first half hour, there is no sign of Russians on the road.

Thinking that nothing interesting will happen I begin to relax until I hear the faint sound of sputtering. it must be the Russians I assume. I run behind a bush hoping I won't be spotted. They are riding in a combat jeep with a large gun on the back. There is a driver, a gunner, and someone who looks to be high-ranking. I take a grenade from my belt without even looking, since I've gotten so used to grabbing them. I pull my pin and aim carefully to judge where the vehicle will be when I throw the grenade. The gunner turns his head to see me getting ready to blow him up, with fear he directs the other soldiers' faces in my direction. The soldier aims his gun at me and loads it. I threw the grenade hoping it would hit the vehicle, but it didn't. It hit the soldier right in the face. The whole combat vehicle blows up along with the soldiers.

Shadow Venom

I feel like taking a few moments to breathe, but I know that I must move on. I continue to hike through the forest as though nothing happened until I come across a deep river. I found three long thick logs and tied them together with some rope I had brought with me. I stand the makeshift bridge up, until placing it close enough to the river edge and letting go. I crossed the river anticipating the idea of ending this whole thing once and for all. Because I am doing this all for my father and Ben. I search relentlessly for a base, but with no reward. I do discover a deer that seems to almost be stalking me. I get paranoid about the deer, so I shoot the thing in the head with my gun. Ending its life. I carry the deer over my shoulder to eat when I return. I grab a few berries and other plants that I find on the way and place them in my bag to eat later.

I see the spark of a flame in the distance. But it's not until I come out of the forest fully that I see that this base is larger than any other one I have ever seen. Most of the other bases have a small surrounding fence of chain or concrete with two towers. Here it must be at least fifteen acres. It is surrounded by a ten-foot chain and concrete fence with barbed wire on the top. With towers all over on the inside. Though it is surrounded by campfires much like the ones at the other bases.

I sneak around the bases to do as I usually do.

I found a small rock the size of my fist. So, I picked it up and threw it at the feet of a lone soldier. He looks down with confusion. Taking the opportunity. I jump onto his back to snap his neck. I dragged his body back into the bush. So, no one spots it. I move on to the next one before noticing there are over ten campfires. When I reach the next campfire, I pull out my katana and ready myself to attack. That's when I noticed this long tree branch sticking out above them.

I try to climb on the thick limbs it provides me with. I nearly slipped on some of the moss, but I managed to make it to the top. Peeking over the branch I can see three men standing below. I take my dagger from my boot and aim steadily at the head of a soldier. I send it flying into the soldier's skull. The other soldier is quick to react and fires his gun up into the sky. I pulled out my shield and jumped from the tree. I grab hold of my katana and stab the soldier in the chest.

Shadow Venom

I relax for a couple of seconds before remembering there were three soldiers. I get shoved to the ground in a matter of seconds after the realization. I got kicked in my side and thrown across the small field. I pulled out my gun as quickly as I could. I was too slow. He grabs hold of my forearm forcing me to slash him with my claws. His grips weakened from the tremendous blood loss pouring from his neck. I don't know what I would do without my weapons. I do know one thing for sure, I wouldn't live very long after attempting combat.

Sneaking through the bushes to the next campfire I decide that I don't want to mess around much anymore, so I pull out my gun and begin to use that to take out everyone. I manage to get through almost every campfire using my gun until I reach the last one and I decide to have a little bit of fun. Seeing as I have worked quite hard this time around.

"So, guys what's for dinner?" I ask while pulling up my shield for protection.

Every soldier jumps in fear. "What? Who's there?" The soldier reacts to me turning white with fear.

Jeremiah Anderson

"It's your good pal Shadow Venom," I say as I charge into the soldier. He doesn't fight offensively, only defensively. I do a quick kick to push onto his back. I use my electrified venom shocker to hit him in the gut and finally use my flame emitter to roast him to death. I see no signs of other soldiers around. So, I moved on to the main base.

I crawl in the tall grassy plain around the guard tower in front of the gate. I shoot two guards with my gun before climbing. I use my claws against the wall to slide down and slow my fall into the base. I hid behind a few vehicles, before taking out a couple of guards. I see moonlight illuminating the area around me so I'm careful to dodge the light since the darkness is my strongest weapon. A dog jumps from out of nowhere, it bites my leg dragging me out of my hiding spot. I'm quick to silence it. I take a good look around and find that there are missiles and other explosives everywhere, all I need is to find the right spot to set off a chain reaction.

Guards are actively patrolling the perimeter. I will have to be as quiet and unnoticeable as possible. I grabbed a few grenades from an open crate I found. I try to grab as many as possible.

After exploring for a few more minutes, I find this large circular center to the base, it has some sort of picture carved into it, but I can't make out what it is. It has a building at the opposite end, it looks like it was placed here yesterday. I look around to see if I find any soldiers. I can't seem to find any, so I crouch down and move slowly into the circle. When I reach the center, I take a quick look around to see if anyone is nearby. Suddenly giant lights flash down on me, lighting up the entire Russian base. Soldiers stand around the perimeter of the circle aiming their guns at me. I look around and know instantly it doesn't matter what I do I won't get out of this one alive.

I saw a figure on top of the building that I was heading for. He looks familiar. "Thought you got rid of me for good huh? Well, let's see who claims victor this round shall we?" It's The Dark Condemner! He lives, he stands before me. He lifts an open palm into the air, then clenches it tight to signal to the soldiers around him to fire. I try to dodge what appears to be tranquilizer darts. Before I can even grab my shield, I am covered head to toe in the darts. I walk around dizzy and unsure of what just happened.

I fall onto the ground with a few more seconds of consciousness, in the realization that I have failed, the Russians might win this thing.

Chapter 8

I wake up alone in a room tied to a chair with a strong thick rope. My suit is gone, and I am weaponless. I notice different types of melee weapons not far from where I am sitting. It's dark and grim here, but it's not too different from my new personality. From what I can tell it's a storage room.

When I was little my father used to lock me up in our shed and leave only a few items for me to use in an escape. I managed to get out every time. But this time even if I escape. I don't have any of my gear. Instead, I'm only wearing a pair of shorts. I can hear people talking on the other side of the door. I attempt to sit as still as I possibly can in the hope that they forget about me. But if they forget about me, how will I get something to eat? Or maybe something to drink?

The door flings open and this older man with a bald head steps into the room. He has many large golden medals on his uniform. He is someone of importance. But he isn't alone. At his side, he has The Dark Condemner and some other man. I think he is some sort of architect judging by what he wears. Also, he is holding blueprints in his left hand.

"So, you are the famous Shadow Venom. I am Colonel Kek Voronin. I have so many questions. Questions that will have to wait. Though I am willing to offer you very good job. It doesn't pay but it keeps you alive. What do you say sport? I heard it is the thing you Americans say. Sport." He giggles like some maniac with the flu.

"Well, first congrats on correct English grammar and slang. Second, I don't take jobs from Russian terrorists. That's pretty much self-explanatory," I say aggravating him.

He looks into my eyes deciding whether to slap me. Or to kill me right off the bat. "Well Okay, I'll tell you what I need anyway. I want you to hunt down every man and woman who wants to rebel against us and kill them. I don't care how just do it. If you refuse there will be consequences," Kek says as a man from behind him walks in with a long taser. I don't particularly like to be tased, but there is no way I can let this man hurt those that I love any longer.

Jeremiah Anderson

"You think you scare me? I've seen your mom without makeup. That's a real horror. There's nothing you can do to scare me or get me to harm even a hair on the head of anyone in my town." I stared into his eyes. They reflect my own. I wish nothing more than to break free of my bonds and slash in in the face.

He grins at me almost amusingly. He makes some hand motions to the man with the taser, causing him to move closer. The man puts away the taser and unexpectedly sends a punch to my face. I think I can guess who the right-hand man is.

Kek grabs my chin and forces it to face him. "Okay, are we ready to cooperate?"

I want to bite every one of his fingers off, but there is still one thing that bothers me. "I have one question. Are you the one who gave the order to blow up Long Beach?" He takes a moment to gather his thoughts as though it's been a long time since it happened.

"Partially, it was more of a team effort. We needed something to make you Americans fear us, we wanted to become your greatest fear."

"Should have just shown us your face."

He shrugs off my comment and doesn't care to instigate back. "Okay, are you ready to work together?"

"No, I will never work with you no matter what happens to me." I feel as though I gave him the idea to torture me into submission. But I don't care. I could never hurt anyone in my town. Anyways once I've done his bidding; he can easily kill me.

"Good, I wanted a show," he says giving me a grin full of mystery and evil. What does he mean he wanted a show?

He leaves the room with The Dark Condemner and the architect, then shuts the door behind him locking it. The soldier who punched me comes from behind and unties me.

I quickly leap over to the weapons stash. I picked up a sword and chopped the soldier's head off. I head for the door, but before I can open it. I hear someone locking it from the other side.

"What? You thought we would let you escape that easy, did you?" He laughs maniacally through the glass. His laughs are full of evil and dastardliness. "Prepare yourself, because at noon you fight." Fight? Fight who. What? Kek walks away with nothing more than a smug grin on his face. I take a quick look at myself, and I find something I haven't seen before. There's some sort of metal band around my forearm. Judging by its placement it's probably used to shock me if I escape. The windows in the back are too small for me to climb out of. And the ones facing the front are too thick.

I hear a loud horn go off not far from where I am. I assume it's just a usual thing, but not long after a couple of men burst into the room holding guns. I jolt at them trying to kill as many as possible, but before even a drop of blood is spilled, I get a shock in my arm. It dazes me for a couple of minutes as they carry me into this large building. Right into another dark and creepy room. When the pain goes away, I push myself up on my feet. I look at some of the weapons here, and I grab a few. I take what appears to be a sickle. I attach a knife holster to myself along with putting a knife or two in them. I notice no ranged weapons are present, which means whatever is about to happen they want to make it as difficult as possible for me. And they certainly want blood. Lots of it.

I hear the same horn again, yet I'm still confused as to what it means. Then suddenly a door behind me rises showing me this large circular room with sand and many strange sculptures made of white blocks. Various weapons are lying around all over, but I'm content with the ones I have already chosen. My chest sinks as fear creeps into my veins. This is not going to be easy. No matter what it is.

"Introducing, the murderer of men. Slasher of soldiers. Shadow Venom!" I hear my name called aloud. I assume I'm supposed to step out at that point. The small crowd around the stadium applauds with joy. There is an opening to the sky above me that I take an interest in. "Introducing, the man who will get rid of our pest problem. Adrick Kim!" The crowd seems more intrigued about this guy than about me. Probably because they know that without my gear, I have almost no chance of surviving. He carries this large, spiked club that's about a yard long and very thick.

After the gates shut, we both walk around the room clockwise, for about a minute, until the bugle sounds. He charges at me looking like some raging rhino. I prepare my stance as he swings at me. I duck and use my sickle to trip him and cut his leg. He falls over into the wall busting his lip. He gets up faster than I could have ever imagined and runs at me again, but as I duck, he dips his club hitting me in the face. Knocking me on my back. He raises his arms in what appears to be victory, but I rush to get up and I climb on a white statue to use it as a backboard to fly at Adrick and stab my sickle in his arm.

Spinning around he throws me against the wall before beating me with his club many times. He picks me up and lays me down in the middle of the stadium and pulls out a knife. He raises it high. Then sends it flying toward my face. But before he can shove it through my skull, I grab my knife and stab him in the thigh as many times as I can before he redirects his knife to the ground. He grabs my arms and uses his control over me to slam me repeatedly into the wall. That's when I noticed the metal band around my wrist. I placed it between me and the wall, and the pressure snapped it in half. Freeing me from the worry of them shocking me to death.

He punches me in the face numerous times before he pins me to the ground. About to send the knife into my chest. He stands up and walks away, allowing me to get up to fight him once more. Acting as though this is some game that he could easily beat me.

Which he probably can.

I pick up a spear and throw it at him, he blocks it almost pathetically. We charge at each other with extreme speed. He throws a punch at me, but I

Shadow Venom

block it easily. I kick his knee throwing it back, before performing a sweep on him. He falls on the ground looking to be mad. I ran for a statue to hide behind. I jump onto the statue and jump off it onto Adrick. I situate myself so my legs are around his neck squeezing life out of him. I pull out one of my knives and raise it to put it through his head, but he flips over making me fly off him.

I hit a statue before feeling extremely dizzy and nearly passing out. He picks me up and slams me into the wall. With each slam feeling as though my skull will break any second. I investigated the seating and noticed Kek laughing his head off. With The Dark Condemner sitting there next to him. Shaking anxiously. I assume he is excited to watch how I die.

Adrick walks away to pick up his club, but when he turns around, he finds I'm gone. He walks around the stadium in search of me. But he can't find me. He begins to lose his mind about how I'm missing, but I carefully shift from Statue to statue hiding behind them. He begins to get so mad he smashes the statues one by one. Until he finds me. With him being in this new and enraged state he shows little to no constraint in charging me to finish me off once and for all. He launches himself at me to grab hold of my leg. He lifts me above his head and slams me against the ground upside down. I can feel the pain in my collarbone from that slam. He spins me around, until hitting me into a statue. I lie on the ground motionless, and in excruciating unbearable pain. Adrick gets closer and closer. He reached for my neck, as I swiftly grabbed my sickle and cut off one of his fingers. He screams so loud Russia can hear him.

His eyes are full of fury as his face turns red in anger and strife. "Why you little..." He reaches down and throws me into the walls again. I nearly unconsciously lie on the ground hoping I can survive this one. If I didn't have weapons I know as a fact I would not win. Adrick suspects this. He picks up all the weapons and places them in his arms and tosses them over the wall. Only a few lay on top of the wall, but most disappear into the seating. "There try cutting off any more of my body parts now!" He yells ready to kill me, but not without a show. I use one of the statues to get back up. I have no weapons other than my brain against his brute strength. The odds are not in my favor.

I get back up, hold my fists to my face, and prepare to die.

Adrick stands in fury and anger with blood spilling from his finger and his thigh. His eyes are darkened, and his face is drowned in the red color that could be either of our blood. His fists are clenched, and his muscles are tensed. He looks at me with those evil eyes and does not break contact. He runs in to tackle me, but I jump thrusting myself off a statue, and land my feet on his face. The kick pushes him into the ground giving me a chance to fight back. I sit on him punching him repeatedly in the face, but my weight isn't enough. He manages to get back up. He throws me over on my back and pins my arms to the ground using his knees. Almost feeling as though someone nailed me down, with actual nails. He just sits there and laughs at me, enjoying my vulnerable position.

I use my legs to pick up a broken piece of a statue and toss it at Adrick's back. He turns his head trying to figure out what hit him. His knees slightly release my hands, but still enough that I can pull them out. As Adrick's' face turns back around, I pick up a rock and hit him in the face with it. He falls on his back cupping his eye. Once he removes his hand, I can see that his eye is broken. I almost threw up at the sight, but this was not the time to do that.

I jump up as fast as I can. Moving back before Adrick can crush me. I threw the rock at him again, but this time he dodged it. He charges at me holding his club. His club hits me in the face and knocks me to the ground. I get more used to the taste of the ground with as many times as I have been pushed down to it. I hope to not have to be put underneath it. With Adrick on top.

Adrick stands above me with his club. I kick his knee, but it does nothing. He seems to be getting stronger with every attack I give him. He raises his club high above me. I know this is the last hit. I can't take another. Or I'll be finished.

When I'm about to accept my fate. I watch The Dark Condemner walk around in the seating area and knock a spear back into the stadium. On the opposite side of the stadium. I swiftly roll out of the way of Adrick's attack. I try to run away, but he grabs me and throws me to the other side of the stadium. I grab hold of the spear and hold it tightly between my bloodshed hands. Adrick approaches faster than he ever has before. Holding his club ready to smash me. He runs at me and throws his club at me. I roll under it and throw the spear at him. I close my eyes for a moment thinking it would miss and that would be the end, but instead, I see it has stabbed right through him.

The victory has brought me strength. The horrible people of the Russian terrorist base deserve to see their champion fall. I grab the spear with both hands to aggressively push it further in. He falls to the ground, not dead but barely alive. I fall to the ground in exhaustion, hoping this is the end. Maybe they will let me out on good behavior. The gate opens back up again. A few men pick me up and drag me back to the chair of fun, where they tie me back up.

Kek walks into the room. Looking about as happy as a kid whose ice cream hit the sidewalk. Along with him The Dark Condemner and a few men enter. "You killed my best fighter. There will be consequences."

"Oh, I'm sorry. next time I'll gladly die for your entertainment," I say sarcastically. I would love to face Kek, I wonder who would win. Old man versus young boy.

"Certainly, make things easier for me," he says smiling gleefully. Not realizing I meant the comment sarcastically.

"If you thought the first round was hard, get ready for the second round," he grins most despicably. He leaves the room signaling others to go with him. The Dark Condemner waits until the others leave before doing anything.

Jeremiah Anderson

"Don't be getting any ideas just because I accidentally knocked the weapon in. You're mine to kill," he says slapping me in the face before leaving. Despite what he says, I feel as though there is something more.

Chapter 9

After not getting very good sleep since I was tied to a chair all night, a man enters the room. He seems to be a doctor because he holds some medical supplies in his hand. He unties me letting me roam free around the room. Showing no fear that I will attack him. Probably because I won't, if he's going to heal me then I might as well let him. He proceeds to wrap the bandage around my hand as I stand around waiting for him to wrap things up. I have been sitting for so long that I can't stand it. He then removes any remaining shards from the statues out of my body. I had to bite my arm because it was so painful. By the time he finishes that part of the checkup. I've already drawn 2 liters worth of blood from my body.

When he finishes, he points to the chair instructing me to sit. He proceeds to tie my hands back up. Then leaving the room. Not once speaking a single word.

Kek enters the room smiling with joy. "Well, how is our little Russian killer?" He must have gotten some good sleep last night.

"Good, and how's our little cosplay Colonel playing god?"

"If I get what I want it won't be for the cosplay." I give him an unsure confused look. Making it obvious that I don't quite understand. "When I take control of your little state, I will continue to move in state by state until taking control of your entire country. I will have so many powerful weapons to the point that I won't be just playing god." The shock of what he says causes me an anxiety attack. What if he finds my mother? He could do any form of torture to her. She might have to fight someone in a stadium like me. "So, I will give you the chance to live. Will you accept my offer to get over your morals and slay your little town? Get your hands dirty?"

"The only thing that's little is your chances of getting me to help you."

He grins in almost pleasure; happy I made that choice. He must have some more deadly game for me to beat.

Shadow Venom

"Well, I hope you have more blood to lose." However, I fear the decision I made. I would rather die than have to kill any innocent. He chuckles as he leaves, and sends another man in. This guy has many things in the bag he carries. I can't make everything out, but I can see a taser and a few saws. He walks behind me making almost no sound, then punching me in the face with a very strong blow. He sends many punches to my face and gut. After having a little fun, he pulls out a taser from his bag and tases me in the back. He continuously shocks me back into reality every time I try to pass out from the blood loss.

He leaves the room and soon returns with large heaters. He places them around me and turns them on the highest setting. He tightens the rope around the chair lessening the chances of me escaping. He then proceeds to leave the room before he can overheat.

~

Sweat pours down my face as I've been sitting here for an hour or two. I struggle to breathe in the overheated air surrounding me. Attempting to use the sweat on my wrists to wriggle out of the rope. I have unsuccessfully tried to escape. The man returns and turns off every heater. At first, I believed that the torture was over, but I couldn't be more wrong. He sends men in to carry my chair with me on it out. He took me to this ice pool. I feel hopeful at first and wonder if maybe he is trying to help me now, but he sets me in the icy water still tied to the chair. With me being unable to move I could freeze. The water feels nice since I was overheating but at some point. It gets cold. Too cold. I shiver in the water, but I try to focus my mind on other things like the location of the moon. I didn't realize it before, but I was probably in the heat longer than I thought, I must have passed out. The moon sits between two trees curved slightly to look as though they're holding it up. I slowly drift away as I start to pass out. Again.

~

I am awake not long after, I can tell because the moon is not far from where it was. I was taken out of the water and moved back to the room to be tied back to the chair. They must have noticed that the rope was getting weaker. Which of course means that they must tie a new one on. I once again begin to believe that the torture is over, but they bring in lights and point them at me. I'm not sure how this is torture at first, but it begins to come together when they place a speaker in the room that plays a horrible sound. When the man leaves the lights shine brightly and the noise machine plays a louder much worse sound. They are attempting to sleep deprive me.

I sit there all night long. Having the lights on me and the noise playing. The man returns and removes the lights and sound machine. He gives me a slight bow as though he is just entertaining me with a show. I try to jump at him from the chair, but the chair weighs too much. I don't even get five minutes of sleep before some soldiers come in and untie me. They surround all sides of me. Escorting me to the battle stadium again. I choose to not look around for any weapons. Instead, I slump over in a corner and fall asleep.

I wake up a few hours later when a bugle sounds, and the gate rises. I don't see weapons around me, so I figure they must be inside. I can hear a voice on the speaker, it must be Kek's.

"Welcome, Shadow Venom. You will be fighting fourteen different men, and if you survive. You will live. If you lose. Death is among the many painful things you will feel."

I take a deep breath and enter the stadium.

Jeremiah Anderson

It has been hours since I've gotten the chance to breathe. I've been fighting for hours. Each one seemed to be a Russian traitor or thief. Or some other convict of theirs. Judging by how they were dressed. Each time I reentered the stadium there was another random assortment of items in there, and each one I had to use to kill the other guy. Like where I had nothing but ropes and had to strangle a guy to death. Or when there were only bricks, and I had to beat the life out of a man.

I am taken back to the room to be checked on by a doctor again, I don't have many cuts, and barely any bruises. These men were not nearly as fast or strong as Adrick.

Kek walks it acting like a hyper kid who had coffee. "Well? How do you feel now? Changing your mind yet? Would you like to be part of our secret organization?" I almost considered the idea, but I know that it's because of the pain that I've had to go through, but that's from the past. Even if the past was only moments ago. I can't accept this deal.

"No, you'll have to kill me before I accept a deal like that." I realize what I just said after I had said it, but at this point, it doesn't matter he's just going to kill me anyway.

Shadow Venom

"That can be arranged," he says smiling maliciously. "Oh, and get this boy some food, he's probably starving." That reminds me I haven't eaten in days, I managed to get water while in the pool of water. But food I've got none of.

Kek holds a loaf of bread in his hands, and waves it in my face, attempting to get a reaction out of me showing my interest in the bread, but I keep my bearing. He tosses the bread on the floor in the corner of the room. Then leaving the room without further remark. I know what he wants me to do. He wishes for me to drag myself and the chair to get the bread. I consider not doing it and protecting my self-dignity. Then I realized, I already lost that when I got captured by a bunch of Russians.

Everyone left me alone in this shed, so I figured I'd use this time to get something to eat. I moved from side to side. Rocking the chair until I hit the ground making a loud thud. I use my feet to thrust the chair through the room across the dirty nasty floor. Nearly getting the bread. As my mouth is going to bite into the bread, Kek returns walking over to me, presenting a grin. Taking the bread and leaving. I lay on the ground motionless for a few minutes, until I found something that caught my eye. There's a sharp rock that might be sharp enough to cut myself free with. I spun the chair around enough to grab the rock. I try to cut myself free before I hear some commotion outside the door. I hear Kek alerting the guards that there will be a very special show tonight and that they are allowed to be relieved of their duties to watch.

The noise soon ends, so I continue to cut the rope until I'm free. I walk over to the door to open it arming myself with the rock, but when I reach for the doorknob, there is none. But there is a metal plate where one would be, I use the stone to carefully pry it off. I look around for something long and skinny enough to fit into the borehole. I didn't find quite what I wanted, but I found some bones. I just hope they are chickens. Not because I'm afraid of what could happen to me, but because if I can't find anything to eat, I might need to chew on that. I sharpen the bone to make it thinner by rubbing it on the concrete floor. Once the bone is in the correct shape. I stick it into the borehole and begin to disconnect the doorknob. I continued until I realized that I only needed to go a bit further until the doorknob could be taken off or turned to allow me the chance to escape. I don't take the chance now. Because if I escape the whole base will go on lockdown and guards will patrol every inch of this place and I won't be able to make it. Plus, I can't fight men with guns like this. I'd die no doubt. But in the probability that the opportunity presents itself. I hid the bone under a few others and hid the rock behind a loose brick.

I pick my chair up to lean it back against the wall. I proceed to tie my hands to the back of the chair, but loose enough to break out if need be. I listen as Kek comes back and talks to the guards. He gives them some more information about tonight's show, then proceeds inside to greet me with his wonderful face.

"Well, how have you been old friend?" His nose wrinkles in laughter and enjoyment as he laughs his way through the sentence. "I hope you have been enjoying your stay." He gives this almost laughable grin as he tries to be sarcastic.

"Not bad. I almost forgot what your face looked like. Maybe next time," I say giving him an arrogant smile while remaining full eye contact without saying another word. He then returns the smile and sweeps the leg of the chair making me hit the floor. I knew if I could get him focused on beating me up, he wouldn't wonder how I was able to get here or figure out that my rope was loose.

Jeremiah Anderson

He stands there laughing at me full of joy. For a cruel man, he sure does laugh a lot. "I would just like you to know that tonight I have something very special for you to fight, and I will allow you to choose one item from your gear to fight them with."

"Yippy, more torture," I say sarcastically.

"How funny we feel the same way about you being in pain, you are one of America's greatest fools, aren't you? No wonder it was so simple to capture you." I became very confused about how he believed I was serious. This man just doesn't get it, does he? "Well, I'll leave you to contemplate how you will spend your final few hours."

"With all the options I don't know how I'll ever choose."

"Have fun," he says leaving the room and giving my ears a rest from his voice. A guard soon enters the room and unties my rope to escort me to the stadium. I see a table lined up with my stuff and a few other items that weren't mine. I consider trying to grab my shield and rush to get my other stuff and fight these guys off, but they are surrounding me, and even if I could take out a few guys. I would be quickly overpowered by the proximity they stand in.

Shadow Venom

I pick up my claws and inspect them deciding if those are what I want. I turn to present my chosen weapon, but before I speak, I see The Dark Condemner shaking his head slowly from side to side almost imperceptibly. I don't know if I can trust him, but I was helped before, so I continue to pick something else. Holding my electrified venom shocker in my hand. I turn my head once again to find him shaking his head, so I move on picking up half my weapons until landing on my flame emitter. I hold it in my hands thinking that if this isn't it, I'm just going to pick what I want instead. And to my surprise, The Dark Condemner nods silently telling me that it's the right choice. I will go ahead and trust him on this. Though I don't trust him at all. But if this is some sort of water stadium, he will be the first guy I kill.

I walk over to Kek with my weapon and hold it before him, he sighs in almost disappointment. "Okay if that's the weapon you choose, so be it." For the first time, he appears to have an outraged anger with me. "Wait until we take our seats and the bugle sounds," he says right before he leaves the room using a secret door. I didn't even know that existed. Maybe I should take a look around.

Jeremiah Anderson

I pace around the room waiting patiently as I wait for the bugle to sound. But when I least expected it, it happened. The bugle sounds and the gate rises. I walk down the hall and find the floor doesn't continue, there's a drop. I move closer to the entrance and look down into the pit.

My heart nearly stops, as I see snakes, spiders, and wasps crawl around in the stadium. I get goosebumps from head to toe, and I shiver like I've fallen into a frozen river.

I'm still fearless, right?

Chapter 10

The creatures below look as though they have been waiting to do nothing more than give me a painful excruciating death. I now understand why The Dark Condemner wanted me to choose my flame emitter. It's the most efficient weapon to wipe out a mass majority of creatures. I resist jumping into the pit so a guard from behind pushes me inside. I fell into the pit and attempted to land on my feet, but when I hit the ground, I fell onto my back. The snakes surrounding me raise their heads in a defensive position. The spiders crawl away in fear. and the wasps don't take any interest in me.

I stand up slowly without any sudden movements, attempting to prevent the snakes from attacking while I work out a plan. I aim for the sky and let the flame show, it scares a decent number of snakes, but not all. Which will work just fine. A snake moves in behind me, so I quickly turn around aim my flame emitter at it, and roast it to a crisp. The other snakes seem to fear me, so they move farther away from me. They appear to be indigo snakes, so if I am bit it shouldn't be deadly. Unless I get too many bites, then that could still cause a severe problem. I take a deep breath and begin to slowly move around the stadium and burn the snakes. Almost the whole area around me has become set ablaze. With burning snakes. Some snakes jump out of nowhere and bite me. They cause pain but no venom is injected, so I couldn't care less.

One snake wraps itself around my leg attempting to constrict it, but I use all my strength to pull it off. One more minute of that and I would need my leg amputated. The other snakes move closer while still being on fire, though most of the snakes have died from the fire only minutes after being set aflame. My shorts begin to catch on fire, but I jump to the ground and put them out on the dirt and sand-mixed floor. I almost forgot about the snakes, but I quickly remember when they started trying to slither on me. I swiftly get back up and do my best to light every snake on fire.

Killing. Every. Last. One.

Taking a moment to breathe, I catch my breath and try to form a new plan for the spiders. As I take a closer look, I believe them to be wolf spiders. They might be slightly trickier than snakes since they are smaller. I draw my attention to a specific set of spiders that are crawling on top of one another looking as though they are trying to burrow themselves in.

I feel a slight itch on my back, when I reach for it, I feel a hairy cover. I know that I don't have back hair, so I grabbed the spider with my whole hand, and I threw it into the wall. Which doesn't appear to do even an ounce of damage to it, it simply gets right back up and stands on its hind legs and growls at me, then all the other spiders do the same. Part of me almost wants to die in that moment. But I just face my fear and begin to light the spiders a blaze. As I'm roasting the spiders a few climb on me delivering a painful bite, it shouldn't kill, as long as I don't get too many bites. I fight each spider off using my flame emitter. The spiders surround me with their mortifying burnt exterior. Only minutes later, they're all dead.

Now I'm surrounded by a thousand dead animal bodies, the only living thing left is the wasps. Wasps are my least favorite, because they can easily attack from any direction, and they don't back down from a challenge. Also considering there's a species rumored to have sting strong enough to kill a cow. I don't want to mess with something that powerful.

Jeremiah Anderson

I gather my courage and take a deep breath to relax before this moment. I tighten the strap on the flame emitter and prepare to activate it. The wasps I do manage to hit, die almost instantly, but most swerve around the flame dodging it. The wasps suddenly stop flying everywhere, they just hover around me. I can tell something bad is about to happen. I almost consider begging for a less painful way to die.

They can't say no if I say please. Right?

The wasps look as though they are communicating until they charge in at me stinging every exposed part of my body. Every sting hurts badly, every inch of me feels the pain, and I almost fall in capitulation. I raise my voice in a rising scream until I can't do so any longer, as I rise to the challenge. Every inch of my body feels the stinging sensation of the stings. They're like hot needles are being driven into me. I'm unable to hit all the wasps at once, so I take out as many as possible by spinning around. The world around me becomes dizzy and begins to black out. I must be close to five hundred stings, which is enough to kill me. I try to focus my eyes as best as I can, but nothing lines up correctly.

The wasps seem to be gathering in a specific spot, it must be their nest. The only reason they are still here. I try to focus enough to stand, but I stumble a few times before getting up. I walk over to the nest and aim at it. I take a deep breath and press the button to activate the flame emitter, but nothing happens. I released the cartage and it's almost empty. I look for something to use, and I find a snake that's still on fire, it should do just fine. I carefully pick up the snake and hold it over the nest. Opening the butane container. I pour it on the snake as I release it from my grip. The snake crushes the nest and traps the wasps underneath it, burning them. My vision slightly returns, but everything is still dizzy. A few wasps are crawling around on the ground, but their wings appear to have been burnt off.

I stumble to the gate, the gate that refuses to open. I turn to look at the crowd, they are all in complete shock. They must have thought I was surely dead. I too thought that I was. I turn to The Dark Condemner, and he gives me a slight nod. The gate begins to rise. Before I can step through, I fall to the ground passing out.

Waking up again in my chair I instantly get shocked back into reality, via the taser in my back. I am greeted with the face of Kek staring me in the eyes, looking as unhappy just as he was the first time that I defeated one of his lackeys. I look down at my chest looking at the wet towels that sit over every sting.

"I didn't want you to heal, but The Dark Condemner insisted. Since what I'm putting you up against next will be your ultimate pain. We want to make sure that you feel the pain," he grins like some hyena that just made a kill. I worry about what I will have to face next if it's worse than what I had to face last time.

"Well long as you enjoyed the show," I say sarcastically.

"You're right, I did enjoy the show. Other than the twist at the end. With you winning. Sport." His nose crumbles and his smile bends in an almost inhuman way. He walks over to the window behind me and peaks out it. I can't tell what he's looking at, but I suspect it can't be good.

"I will give you one more chance, if you choose to not accept then no matter what happens, you will not see the light of day again. Would you like to get over your foolish morals? And fight for me? I promise if you accept you and your loved ones won't be harmed."

Shadow Venom

"Not on my father's grave," I say staring deep into his eyes, knowing well that he would instantly kill me if not torture me after he gets what he wants. I would rather die now than later. After innocents have been killed.

"So be it, you will die tomorrow evening."

"Great, and I'll pick the color for my sixteen-layer cake."

"Do Americans really have sixteen-layer cakes at funerals? Wow, I have much to learn about your country. Since I plan to overthrow it." I don't know what makes this dude think he can overthrow America, considering he only has a small army compared to thousands of American soldiers. However, if he gains enough land, Russia might come to help him complete his plan.

Kek leaves the room without any further comments, but moments later it opens again with The Dark Condemner entering, he lifts this bottle of water to my mouth insisting I drink some. I open my mouth enough for him to pour water in, but I watch him the whole time. Afraid that he's going to shove a knife into my gut.

Jeremiah Anderson

"Fantastic job," he says placing the lid back on the bottle, before leaving again. He's been helping me a lot during my imprisonment. I almost hate to have to kill him after I hopefully escape this place.

I don't know what this next challenge will be, but I need to relax my mind as much as possible. I try to think about memories to help comfort me in the state I'm currently in. I recall a time when My father, Ben, and I hiked through the very woods I'm trapped in now. To go hunting. We spent the whole afternoon trying to catch a deer. We were unable to catch any, so we were moving along a river to see if we could find any signs of deer. While we were walking this stone below my father came loose and he fell into the water. When he climbs out, I hear nothing but him screaming. Then he falls back into the water. I couldn't figure out why until I saw a timber rattlesnake slithering away back into the woods. I dive into the water and lift my father to the surface. Ben grabs him and lays him down on the smooth rocks.

"You know what to do Hunter," Ben says reassuring me that I need to focus instead of worrying about whether my father will die. My father's phone was at the bottom of the river and unusable, so I had to run through the forest jumping every bush and fallen log, until I ran four miles to the opening of the forest. I hop on my motorcycle and ride back into town to the nearest clinic to get help for my father. They get a helicopter ready to get over to the site of the bite. The ride takes about ten minutes before getting to my father, they load him into the helicopter as carefully as possible. I thought I was going to lose him that day.

That was when I knew losing him would be my greatest fear.

My daydreaming ends when my door flies open, with Kek on the other side. The last thing I need right now is his face in mine. "Prepare yourself Shadow Venom, tomorrow you die." I could care less about what he says since I've won every one of his challenges and I'll beat this one too.

"I am prepared, even if I do die, there are plenty more men who can stop you." I think of how Mark can come and destroy this guy and his small army. I have tried to avenge my father and Ben. Perhaps I will need to be avenged next.

"You're the only one who has gotten close to stopping my operation, and even then, you've still failed. I will see you tomorrow," he says stomping his foot down in anger. He leaves the room for what may be the last time, but I try to be optimistic. Something I haven't been in a while and hope that things will turn out the way I wish for them to. I will try to get some sleep tonight since whatever I am going to face tomorrow probably won't be fun. Since I nearly died from the last one, if this one is as bad as Kek makes it sound. I can't even imagine.

I woke up a little after noon. I'm able to tell because of the watch that the guard is wearing. He unties me from the chair and walks me to the stadium. The room I'm dropped off in has dummies everywhere and all sorts of weapons. I even find my clawed gloves on a table, along with my shield and my other weapons. I hear the bugle sound, so I assume this is it. The day I possibly die. I quickly strap my weapons to me and prepare for this ultimate danger. The gate rises once again, letting me see the stadium. I slowly enter and see that this time wooden poles are coming from the ground, with sand everywhere. I see nothing that would immediately put me in danger. I started to wonder if he was trying to bluff me into believing he had something so dangerous that I would kill myself before entering.

"Well, where is it? Where is my ultimate pain?" I yelled to Kek. I look over to The Dark Condemner to see if he will give a response, but he just looks down at his feet. I look around the stadium for some danger, but I see nothing. Until I see two boys holding knives, I can't make them out until I get closer. It's Matthew and Markus from my neighborhood. What are they doing here? How did they get here? I would have thought that they were killed by The Dark Condemner.

It takes a few seconds for it to render, but when it does it shocks me. This is what my ultimate pain is…

I must kill my friends.

Chapter 11

I stare into their scared eyes as they stare into mine. I approach them slowly and try to talk to them. "Hey you guys, okay?" I try to stay calm hoping they will have a similar response.

"Well, I'm not so sure I feel that great at the moment, since it looks like we have to kill each other. Also, with what they said about your fighting skills. I don't think I would want to engage in a fight with you," says Matthew, looking like a scared puppy, without having a clue about what to do. Even though the obvious thing for him to do is fight. But he refuses.

"Well, we can try to find a way out of this," I say. I don't think there is any way out of this… This must be it. But to deliberately kill my friend, all for the cause of avenging my father as well as Ben. So, if I were to kill them, I'd have to kill myself. To avenge them from me. Their killer.

Shadow Venom

"No, we have no chance out of this alive. You're the only one who has any chance of escaping, and killing those Russian terrorists," Markus says with such strength that I've never seen him use before. They look at each other and give a nod. I've never understood how these two can communicate using nothing more than a nod.

They raise their knives to their necks and start to slice before I pull their hands back. "What are you doing?" I say anxiously, they must think I'm more than capable enough to stop these Russian terrorists. But the truth is either way I'm dead.

"We want to end things quickly, not only do we know you would win. But you deserve to win."

I don't deserve to win. I'm a wreck right now, my father's gone. So is my best friend. I can barely hold my emotions together. So, I unleashed my wrath on the Russian terrorists that took the life of my father. My mission isn't over until the blood of those Russian terrorists is spilled on my blades.

"You need to go on, fight these guys," Markus insists. "We would rather die now, than a painful death later at the hands of the Russians. We choose our fate; others do not decide our choices. We are the only ones that can choose, the change is up to us. Others do not decide what is right and what is wrong," Markus exclaims. I stand here frozen in front of him, not sure what to make of what he said, staring endlessly into his eyes.

"Well, I don't know what you want to do, but I'm going to get you guys out of this alive, if it's the last thing I do," I say. I don't want them to die, or else their blood is on my hands. Is that all I'm afraid of?

Guilt?

I don't feel at all worried about how they feel right now. Knowing no matter what they couldn't beat me, and that no way will they be able to see their loved ones again.

They both communicate in a simple nod and ready their stance. "If you won't let us rid ourselves for the greater good, then we'll just fight you first to stop you from stopping us," Mark states.

"Then I'll win and stop you from making a poor decision," I say, hoping that they will listen to reason. They both ran towards me, attacking from different sides aiming primarily for my legs. I duck from under Markus's punch and sweep Markus on his back. Now I focus on Matthew.

Shadow Venom

"Matthew please, don't do this," I know he will keep going no matter what I say, but I continue to stop him anyway.

"No, this is how I want it to end, avenge us."

"I'm sorry," I hear Markus say from behind me, I think nothing of it at first until I feel the sharp pain in my calves. Markus stabbed his knife into my calves. I fell to the ground unable to stand from the pain. Markus walks over to Matthew, and they look as though they are never going to see each other again. They raise their knives, seemingly about to pierce their chests, but they don't. They stab each other in the heart.

"No!" I scream in terror and sadness, as I watch two friends of mine die in front of me. I sit helplessly with the both of them. I could have saved them. I know I could have. Anger rises in me knowing I've just lost two dear friends of mine. And it's not only Keks fault but mine as well, I should have stopped them.

"Please... pull... out... the knife," Markus says to me in his final breath. I remove the knives from their chests to quicken the death, but at this point what does it matter?

Jeremiah Anderson

A few tears escaped from my eyes before I heard the gate rising again. Guards drag me out as I scream at them, asking them to help my friends. But they became tired of my screaming and shut me up with some sedative that they forced into my arm with a needle, causing me to black out. If I don't escape soon then I will be at Keks mercy for any torture.

I need to escape tonight.

I wake up startled back in my chair by an electric shock into my back, the guard who shocked me steps around the side of the chair and punches me in the face. I begin to recognize his face, but it's not until he steps into the light that I figure out who it could be, it's the man who instructed all those torture techniques on me a couple of days ago.

"Nice to see you too, I've missed the pleasure of your company," I say sarcastically, getting nothing more than a genuine smile in return. He proceeds to walk out of the room and returns with a few pieces of wood. He nails the wood into the wall, blocking light from entering the room. By the time he's done, I can barely see a thing.

I spend a couple of hours like that until he returns to have some more fun, he brings in his heaters again amping them up to the max, and leaves me in the room like that. I sweat for hours upon hours, until the power goes off, and I hear banging on the window behind me and a fresh breeze lets in.

"Hey son, it's me Mark, I'm here to get you out," he must have been looking for me since I hadn't communicated in a few days, and I felt a sense of joy come upon me.

"Thanks, but I can't fit through that window and even if you get me out now, I don't have my gear, so I won't be able to fight these fiends." I talk fast but soft enough that no one else should hear.

"Okay, would a batch of explosives do well enough?"

"Yes, those should do," I say exhilarated. I may have a plan that could work if I can get those guards to get away from the door. Mark pulls the board back into place to hide the window, making the room dark once again. I plan how to get the guards away as I wait patiently for Mark to return with the explosives. If the guards don't talk then I can hear everything through the walls, the trees blowing in the breeze, the birds chirping, or the faint sound of a coyote. I listen to the sounds of nature until I hear someone approaching the door.

Jeremiah Anderson

The guards stop talking instantly. I fear that it is Kek coming back to give me another painful torture. "Why hello, how are you?" The Dark Condemner asks. He enters the room, acting stranger than usual.

"Been better," I state while rolling my eyes. He closes the door and moves in closer to me. I cautiously move my knees, so they are both pointing in his direction. In this case, he tries to attack.

"They plan to do something with you, I'm not quite sure what. But they are going to do something you can't win at. I want to help you escape. Though I have a bone to pick with you. I will do everything in my power to prevent them from hurting you."

I can't quite tell why, but he seems quite genuine. Like he knows me and genuinely cares for me, but no one I know would do the things he's done. I'll at least have a better shot at living with him on my side.

"Okay, and what do you get in return?" I decided to ask him since for all I know I'm not the only prisoner here.

"Nothing, I'll find a different way out, you're not the only one kept prisoner here. There are far too many captives here. I'll try to help them escape as well." I am right he's trapped here like me. I don't know how he will escape alive, but I'll trust he knows what he's doing. "I'll take out the guards at midnight. Not like you would know what time that would be, but you will hear a cannon go off at eleven-thirty tonight. Don't ask me why eleven-thirty, just go with it."

"Okay, will you open the door?"

"No, you need to request a key, and if it's not returned by the time of shutdown. There will be consequences, and I won't be allowed to get one tonight," I can't quite tell why, but I feel a sense of trust in him I haven't felt in a little while.

"Midnight!" He shouts as he leaves the room, leaving the door slightly open. Enough for me to escape tonight. I heard some commotion outside, I wondered what it could be, but two seconds later I got my answer.

"Hello Shadow Venom, I hope you have enjoyed your stay. Because you won't be here much longer. You're going to take little trip to Motherland, you're going to Russia," he said as he gave this smile as though he thought he'd won. I may not have complete faith in The Dark Condemner, but I do in Mark.

"I've always wanted to ride a polar bear," I say, trying to distract him. If I distract him enough maybe, he will forget to shut the door all the way.

"Oh, but you won't be allowed to go very far, you will be put in a cage outside in the cold, wearing no more than you are now, and forced to eat food and drink water, and if you're lucky you get small cloth as blanket." Wow, he makes everything sound as though I'm going to live in a zoo. Which is basically what it is.

"I guess I'll have to survive there too, after all, I survived you." I know very well that I will not survive in that place, they refuse to let anyone starve themselves to death, or dehydrate. It's pure torture.

"Good luck, and I do mean it," he says as he slams the door shut. The door I planned to escape from. I ponder how to open the door, before remembering I can use the rocks I found, the only problem is I can't untie myself. It's too dark to find another rock to cut myself with, but maybe if I can hold out until Mark gets back, he can get me a knife.

I wait patiently for Mark to return with everything I need for my escape, and for the cannon to go off alerting me that The Dark Condemner will attack soon. But I'm starting to wonder if The Dark Condemner is trying to mess with me.

Boom! The cannon goes off, and at that moment the window bursts open. "It's me, Mark, I have everything you might need to escape. I would go around and fend off the guards, but I'm outnumbered." He must have wanted to wait for a loud sound to break the glass.

"It's fine, I have a guy on that. Do you have the explosives?"

"Yes, was there anything else you needed?"

"A knife would be nice." He climbs down from the window. Then reappears a few minutes later with a knife.

"Hold on one second," Mark says reaching into his pocket, "here catch," Mark says as he throws a knife into my hands. It nearly slipped from my grasp, but I caught it as it cut my hand. I keep my grip on it and begin to cut myself loose.

"Thanks, Mark, that should be all I need." Mark climbs down from the window before a guard catches him. I can hear the guard asking him questions, but that ends fast because Mark gives up and begins running within seconds.

Stumbling over to the brick that I hid my rock behind; I almost passed out from being so tired. I removed the brick from the wall and quickly went over to remove the metal plate from the borehole. I finish fast, but I'm still not free to go. I hear muffling from on the other side of the door, I assume The Dark Condemner is dealing with them for me. Moments later it stops. I stepped outside to find all the guards on the ground. A loud thud bangs against the ground from behind me, I get startled by this sound and jump grabbing a gun. Upon closer inspection, I find it to be a bag, with all my gear. Locked and loaded. I look up to find The Dark Condemner on the roof.

"Don't mess it up," he says right before disappearing out of my line of sight. I understand what he means. If I fail not only, will it put him in danger of being discovered helping an enemy, and I will most likely have to suffer an even more painful death sentence than I'm already in.

I suited up and prepared to escape this place. I picked up a few grenades and lined up the inside of the building I was trapped in with the explosives. I unpin a grenade and at a safe distance, I throw it in. The minute the explosion went off sirens began and suddenly I felt like I was in for more than I thought. Men are patrolling every little speck of dust in this place, I won't make it out of here without being seen, that I do know. But who says I can't have a little fun since I've been trapped in my little Russian prison? I find a few lone soldiers and I take them out by slitting their throats with my daggers. I sneak up on a few more soldiers and I roast them to death. That's when I realized, those weren't the guys I wanted.

I wanted Colonel Kek Voronin.

I make my way to the largest building in the housing unit, where I assume Kek would be. I smash the door open and make my way upstairs to his room. The first door I open I find screaming little girls in the room, I quickly shut it. Hoping that didn't set him off that I'm coming for him. That is if the loud sirens didn't. The next door must be his room, it has a gold lining that is certainly his. I open the door and find him on his bed holding a gun at the door, he fires it at me, but I'm too quick in response. I dodge it without even thinking.

I hold a gun in one hand and a shield in the other. "Stay away from me you... you... you demon in the night." Kek's voice trembles at my presence. He knows that of all things I won't show mercy on him. He seems genuinely terrified of me; I mean I would be of me too. He knows it's over. But rather, it's a question of how.

"Ready to feel somewhat of the pain I've had to feel?" I ask aggressively shaking in so much anger I feel as though I'm about to pass out. I move closer to him, but he continues to fire at me even though my shield is deflecting all his bullets. I get tired of his shooting, so I fire a bullet into his hand. Enabling him to be unable to shoot his gun.

"Please, I'll give you whatever you want... anything." he's nothing more than a man in fear. He's making false deals, trying to escape his imminent death. Though he deserves every drop of blood that is removed from his body.

"No, you had the choice to not send that bomb, but you did. Now you will pay for your crimes." I want to cause him unending insufferable pain, but I can't stay forever, so I must make it quick.

"Please, I'm only the chief of this base," he says shifting from a cry for mercy to a laugher. "There are many more men that will take control and continue what I have started. So, you will never win." he begins to laugh maniacally, coughing up blood.

Shadow Venom

I've decided enough is enough, so I grabbed a rope from his room. I use it to tie a noose and drag him over to his terrace then I wrap it around his neck. After tying the other end to a pillar. I lift him above the terrace, and I throw him over. I hear the scream of a woman in the room below as she watches Kek being hung to death. I found this long rope extending to the outside of this base, so my best guess is that this was an escape plan for Kek if the base was infiltrated. I head for the rope, but I like to leave with a bang. I look for some explosives around the room, but I nearly give up until I search under his carpet, and I find a loose floorboard with all sorts of deadly explosives below. I place them all around the room, and I store a few in my bag for myself. I used a timed bomb so I could focus more on escaping, and I set it for ten seconds. I run for the rope, hoping there will be enough time. I grab this metal bar that is bent enough that it should work to slide down the rope. I stand on the terrace and jump as I slide down the rope to freedom the bomb goes off blowing up the house. However, I do wonder, what if the rope blows? Guess it won't matter at this point.

I make it to the other side of the wall before hitting the ground, finally able to smell the wonderful smell of freedom once again.

Jeremiah Anderson

Chapter 12

I walk through the forest in the damp swampy terrain. Which agonizes my feet. But it's still better than still being in the Russian prison base. It takes a few hours to reach the last place I left my motorcycle, and I'm unsurprised to find it completely drenched by the river. Many sticks and logs have fallen over the motorcycle, crushing the handlebars and front fork. I unfortunately won't be able to ride home with it, so I will leave it here.

I would spend time grieving over the fact that this was my father's, but after all I've been through. I don't think he would care.

I spent a half hour collecting some berries since I hadn't eaten anything in so long. I could occasionally get water when the roof leaked. After collecting food, I continue to the edge of the forest, where I find a few Russian combat jeeps. With me away they must have taken the opportunity to get farther into town. All the men who operate the jeeps lay aside sleeping in their tents. I unclip a grenade from my belt and hide in a bush concealing myself from any onlookers who might want me dead. I threw the grenade at the most distant jeep. Blowing it up and waking the soldiers. They flood out of their tents like ants, yelling at each other in Russian. I quickly unclip a few more grenades and throw them under a few more jeeps.

One blows sky high, landing on top of a soldier's tent. Killing anyone left inside.

The other soldiers scream at each other trying to figure out what happened, while I'm busy blowing things up. They all hop in the final jeep, attempting to ride off back into the forest. But I accurately threw a grenade into the road, blowing up the jeep from underneath.

After blowing the life out of the Russians. I headed back into town to get home. When I reach the greeting sign in the neighborhood, I find it to be smashed into the ground. As I proceed to enter the neighborhood, I find many houses either completely blown up or some that are only partially blown up. Worry hits me, my mother could be in danger, hurt, or worse. I would rather her death over being captured, she would surely die a painful death. I run with all my strength to get home when I get there, there's nothing left.

Shadow Venom

Not even a piece of wood lying on the ground of ash. They must have figured out who I was and sent bombers to blow up the place. They must have blown up half the neighborhood as a punishment.

What have I done? I worry in my head, the thoughts shooting in and out of my mind a million times, before deciding that I need to gain help from Mark and the Strike Back Stingers and finish this war.

I have no way to get there fast without my motorcycle, but I have something that might work. My father used to hide weapons and other gear around town so if something got out of hand while he was off duty, he could easily get his stuff. I run for the town grocery store, where I work.

~

It takes a long time to get there without my motorcycle. But when I do arrive, I'm ever so happy to find my father's shed around the back. A long time ago the store owner couldn't afford the price of land anymore, so he realized that he would have to sell. My father loved the store because it was a good communal place to be. So, my father bought a small piece of land a little off to the side, the worst land property he ever bought, I thought until today. He stored some gear in here, including his motorcycle. I hopped on and rode off to the old warehouse, where Mark and the rest of his resistance should be.

When I reach the warehouse, I don't hesitate to climb up the wall and through a window. When I get to the bottom, I find that this place has grown more than it had the last time I was here. It has most of the neighborhood here, and they are lying in medical beds. Being taken care of by doctors. They must have been injured in the bombing. I look everywhere for my mother, but it's not until a group of people separate themselves from their injured elders that I see my mother staring at me, with her beautiful blue eyes. She has tears running down her face, but it takes every fiber of her being to not run at me and hug me. She knows with me still being suited up my identity could be given away, and that can't happen. It could put me at more risk. I give her a nod, as I continue walking to see Mark.

I walk down the hall to find rooms filled up with different things such as food, weapons, explosives, map rooms, and the Strike Back Stingers suit-up room.

When I got to the office, I found Mark sitting at a desk asleep. "Hey man wake up, wake up!" I yell to Mark, he only moves around enough to adjust in his chair, before falling back asleep. I walk over to him to pick up his cup of water, and I pour it on his head. Causing him to jolt up like he heard a big sale was going on.

"What was that for, son?" He looks at me with confusion and anger in his eyes.

"I wanted to thank you for everything you did for me. I wanted to know if I could return the favor." Mark looks at me as though he's ready to throw something at me, before calming down and sitting back in his chair.

He looks at the ground and gives a little smile, before looking up at me. "You're very welcome son, you've done a good job. Though there is one thing I need you to do for me."

"Name it." I may regret whatever he is asking, but he saved my life.

"I need some information from a few Russian soldiers, they refuse to give us information." He knows that I could probably get information out of a pig.

"I think I can do that." I immediately start thinking of all the painful tactics I can use to get information out.

Jeremiah Anderson

"Try to stay humane." He looks at me as though he can read my thoughts. Knowing I want nothing more than to make those Russians suffer.

"I can promise you this, it will be painless... for me." he slouches back into his chair looking at the wall away from me, knowing he made a bad decision for choosing me of all people to extract information without killing a man.

I leave the room without any further speech before he can change his mind. I walk a little farther down the hall until I find a few metal doors with bars on them and guards in front of them. "I was requested to interrogate a prisoner, please step aside." The guard looks at me with a puzzled face, deciding whether to trust me. After about a minute of that, he decides to let me in to interrogate.

I enter the cell and find the prisoner in the corner motionless with his arms around his knees. "Get up, sit in the bed. Now!" I say in an inhumanely evil voice. He turns his head and runs for his bed instantly. I sit across from him, staring into his eyes, he recognizes who I am, and fears me. He begins to spill all the information he can give me on the bases and their weak spots. He didn't give me any new information, but he did show that he fears me, so maybe his other buddies may fear me the way he does. I leave the room before I scare him into trying to escape. The next room has a man tied to a metal chair bolted to the ground. He struggles to escape the chair, he shakes intensely trying to escape, but he has no success. He screams out loud, seemingly for no reason.

I figure I might as well try to find out what I can. "So, what information can you give me?" I asked him, ready to take my knife and stab it into his heart.

"I don't speak to incompetents."

"Really? Well then, I guess if you refuse to talk, we are going to have to do this the fun way." I grab my dagger and slowly walk over to him. I gradually cut into his thigh. He resists the pain and takes it like a man until I reach a tendon. That's where he gives in.

"Okay fine, fine I'll talk. But don't you dare put that knife anywhere near me again," he exclaims gasping trying to keep in his screams. Most of what he tells me is what I already knew. I began to leave, but then he told me something I didn't know. "There are ships along the beach. We use them to transport troops from Russia to here, we chose this state because it was one of the last spots that we believed people would expect us to attack."

"I think I've gotten the information I need for the day." I move on to the final room, which has two guards at the door instead of one. I wonder who or what could be behind that door. I walk closer to the door, and peaking inside I find a man that I did not expect, Dmitry Slovak. I walked into the room to find him in a cage chained to the wall, with an iron clasp around his neck. He doesn't even care to acknowledge that I have entered the room, he simply ignores me to stare at the black floor.

"Why are you here?" I ask him, expecting some sort of smart-aleck response, but he doesn't even reply. I walk closer to him pressing my hands and elbows against the bars that keep him contained in the cage, looking at his back with scars on them.

"What happened, were you hurt during interrogation?" I asked him but no response was given by him. I became frustrated with him.

"Were you riding your bike without training wheels for the first time, and got a boo-boo?" He still refused to respond. I tried one last time.

"You had a watch, but it was taken years ago, what happened?" He finally turned to look at me.

"How do you know that? That that I had a watch?"

"I'm psychic, I'm the one asking the questions."

"Well since you're psycho you should know that I was in the middle of eating my lunch when I got a call to go to the visiting center. I never get visitors, so I knew something was up from that point. I went anyway, and I saw this kid sitting at the table I was meant to sit at. I asked him why he came to see me, and he told me that he needed my watch. I told him no. He just looked at me and glared for a few minutes, no communication. Then when we got the call that visiting hour was over, he got up and hugged me, I didn't like that, so I shoved him back. Then guards came to get me and took me back to my cell. When I got back, I went to wash my hands, and I found my watch to be missing, so I called up some guys to rough the kid up, but I never got my watch back."

"Such a heartfelt story it's cute and adhering. So why the scars on your back?"

Jeremiah Anderson

"The Russians whipped me, though I am one of them. They told me I spent too much time in the Americas, so I am one of you not one of them. When I came to offer my help to your resistance, they locked me up. To be fair I did escape prison."

"Okay I've heard enough, have a nice day." I leave the room before I begin to feel bad for him, though he is an evil man, he's got human emotions. I headed back to Mark to tell him the new information, but he didn't appear too interested at the moment. he's on a phone call and it doesn't look like things are going well.

"What? You lost twenty-four men! Draw back now, before you lose more, no, no you need to come back. Now!" He must be having some trouble sending men to take out bases. I presume from what I heard that he's having heavy losses. He hung up the phone moments later, turning to me. "Get anything?" He says smiling like nothing happened, but I can see the sadness in his eyes.

"Yes, they are using ships to transport troops from Russia to America. I assume along Long Beach."

"Okay good, I'll send a team."

Shadow Venom

"No, no need. I'll do it."

"You can't, not with all these bases still here, we need to take them out before messing with the ships."

"But taking out the ships would limit the number of resources they can use the rebuild, and they won't be able to get more people over."

"Yes, that's true, but while you were busy playing with your Russian friends. They set up bases everywhere along Long Island, and there are over eighteen total bases throughout the forest. Bases first."

"Yes sir, I will get on it as soon as possible."

"No, you need to eat for now, regain strength, and go tomorrow night."

"Yes sir," I respond showing my newfound respect for him. I leave the room and walk down the hall with nothing but determination to finish off these Russians. I find a room with clothing in it, and I take some that are my size, and I sneak into a closet. I changed my clothes, so I'm not Shadow Venom anymore, now I'm good old Hunter Conners. I look for my mother, to greet her and let her know I'm okay. My eyes almost instantly lock with hers, before running into her arms like I'm about to lose her, for all I know I am.

"I love you so much, please be more careful, or no more parties, you're lucky Mr. Mark found you," she says holding me in her arms trying to savor the moment. But it ends when she notices all the cuts on my arms along with stings, bites, bruises, and burns. I must not have noticed when I was imprisoned. I had more to worry about then. She sits me down on a bed and places bandages on me. She pulls off my shirt revealing many more cuts and scars I have. She glares at me but ends up in a smile showing though she's mad, she's still happy I'm not dead.

What would I do without my mother?

Chapter 13

After my bandages have been placed all around me, I stand up to look for

Chloe. After all, she is my date for the dance. If there is one. I walk around

the injured patients that lie either on the ground or in beds, some of them

have lost their sight and reach out to grab me, hoping I will stay with them.

But I can't.

When I find Chloe, she has her head resting on top of her arms against a

bed. With tears running down the sides of her face.

"Hey, you, okay?" I ask, sitting down next to her. Her head turns to me

slowly, and after taking a few seconds through the tears, she begins to

recognize me. This huge smile comes upon her face, with her eyes twinkling

in the light.

"Hunter, I thought you died in the attack," she says crying more as she wraps her arms around me giving the biggest hug I've ever been given.

"Well as you can see, I'm alive, boy I thought you were crying about something truly awful."

"Losing you is truly awful; I've already lost one best friend I can't lose another." If only Chloe, Ben, and I could have had the chance to say goodbye. I wish I could tell Chloe what I've been doing, but it would put her in danger. If they were to discover her connection to Shadow Venom, she could get killed.

"I… I need to go do something okay? I will see you later," I say as she gives me an almost imperceptible nod, barely letting me go from her grasp. I get up and head back to the closet my suit is in.

Suddenly I hear this rumbling and yelling coming from the hall, I stop to listen, as it gets stronger and stronger. Mark along with other men are running down the hall, but why? I watch as men fall for seemingly no reason until I see three men in the Strike Back Stinger suits. Mark and the other men run and hide behind some crates taking cover, as they attempt to shoot at the attackers. Chloe grabs my hand and pulls me under the bed.

Shadow Venom

"No, you are staying here it's too dangerous," she warns me fearing my safety. I lean in and kiss her on the forehead. Before she can stop me, I pull myself out from under the bed to run and hide behind a crate myself. I realize that I'm being inconsiderate about the fact Chloe is afraid for me and doesn't want me to leave. But everyone has a purpose in life and mine is to protect those that I care about. By any means necessary.

After close inspection of the threat, I realized that there was no way to run through them and get to my suit without dying. So, I need an alternative way to reach the top. I look up and spot a ladder that leads to a bridge above the enemy. I quickly ran for the ladder, but before I reached the ladder I tripped over a pile of rope. It stopped me from getting hit by the oncoming bullets, so I don't complain.

I climb the ladder, climbing high to the bridge to run across it and jump through a window giving me access to the roof. I search around until I find a stairwell leading back inside the building when I do I go down and run down the hall as fast as I can. I ran past the rooms where the prisoners were held, but they weren't there anymore. That's when I realized that I was in real danger now.

Jeremiah Anderson

When I got to Mark's office the whole room had black char everywhere from some explosives. I need to hurry. I find three of the Strike Back Stingers suits missing, the prisoners must have escaped and decided to go on a rampage. I finally get to the men attacking everyone, I distinguish who is who by their voices. I decided to leave Dmitry alone and shoot the others in the back of the neck. Dmitry turns around and aims to fire his gun at me, but before he can pull the trigger, Mark jumps onto him and stabs him in the back. Dmitry falls to the ground without saying a word. He must have realized he wasn't going to get far and figured it was easier to go along with the arrest rather than resist.

Mark walks over to me looking very concerned for me. "You okay kid? You shouldn't be fighting things that are greater than you are, know your place," he tells me, giving me a quick wink to let me know he's only putting on a show. But he isn't wrong because I should have slipped my suit on.

"Yes sir," I say giving him a respectful response to show I understand and am playing along. I move on to check on people. I look for Chloe first since she's the closest, I look under her bed where I last saw her, to find her trembling with fear.

"I'm sorry I had to leave you, they needed help."

Shadow Venom

"They could have fought without you." Little did she know they could not have; they were pinned behind some crates. With no way of fighting back without dying.

"Okay, I understand, can you forgive me?"

She picks her head up from under the bed and gives me her beautiful smile and proceeds to hug me. "Of course." When I finish things up with Chloe, I go to find my mother, but I don't approach her since she's dealing with bullet wounds helping the doctors and nurses. Heading back to the closet to get my gear, I suit up and get ready to head out and scout out the area of these bases. With all the chaos right now, Mark won't be able to tell.

Right when I'm about to climb out of here, Mark runs up to me. "I needed to let you know something. You can take out as many bases as you want, but make sure you try to remember which ones you take out, also I've had reports of a suspicious figure inside an old warehouse not far from here. Check it out."

"Sure thing," I say giving him a quick nod and continuing to climb out of the current warehouse I'm in. He must have suspected that I would refuse to wait until morning. I started up my father's motorcycle without any hassle since this one isn't like a million years old like mine.

~

I won't stop riding until I reach the warehouse Mark told me about, I recognize it, it's the same one that I noticed a figure in a couple of weeks ago. I wonder if there is any correlation. I park my father's motorcycle near a tree that has grown out of the cracks in the concrete. I slowly walk closer to the building, being weary of any attack that could come my way. My shield is around my arm and my claws ready with my hand wide open ready to slit the neck of any man willing to attempt to take me on. Pushing the door open, I find a tidy floor inside. The building hasn't been in use for a long time, I wonder curiously who could be here. Continuing to wander upstairs to the second level, the place still looks clean for something that hasn't been in use for years. When I reach the top, I find a tent and a mini fridge, with piles of food, and a heater. Someone's certainly been here. Judging by the soft breadcrumbs on the floor, someone was here not long ago.

As I'm about to look inside the tent I hear wooden planks fall behind me, I look to see if anyone is there, but I don't see a single living thing. Aside from moss and other plants that have overgrown inside this place. Looking up I spot a hole in the roof that the planks came from. I rush to the next level, checking for a Russian soldier who may be trying to kill me. I still don't see anyone, except the only person who has tried to kill me almost every time we've met, but also the person who saved me.

The Dark Condemner.

"Have you come to kill me? Come to get revenge for me killing your best friend?" He seems to be so relaxed, maybe he's trying to trick me into a false sense of security. But how does he know that he killed my best friend, he killed many people he's probably only assuming.

What can he possibly know?

"You know I can't let a vicious killer like you run free," I get ready to charge at him and push him off the roof, I place my left leg back and turn on my electrified venom shocker.

"Hunter, you need to listen to me, I…" How does he know my name? It doesn't matter. I run at him before he can say another word, I throw a punch with my left hand at him, but he just ducks and it misses him completely. My swing was too strong, I began to tumble off the roof. This is it, because of my rage I'm going to die. But before I make it fully off the roof, I feel someone grab my arm and pull me back up, it's The Dark Condemner. Then again, he is the only other person here.

"I need to talk to you, listen to me," he commands. I ignore him. Because I don't want excuses.

"No, you killed my best friend!" I yell at him as though it matters if I reply, though it does not. I will have his head soon.

"Listen!" He says as I go to throw a punch to his face again, I aimlessly miss, as he bends down and tackles me shoving me to the ground.

"You need to listen, I am…"

"Going to die," I respond, flipping him over onto his back. I relentlessly punch him, not holding back a single punch from connecting with his face or chest. He becomes angrier with me by the second, kicking me in the gut and throwing me off him. Almost as though he could predict my next move, he grabs my hand as I reach for my dagger and stops me before I can get a gun.

"Listen to me!" he screams once again, expecting me to stop what I'm doing and yield. I will never stop until I have wiped out every Russian on

Shadow Venom

American soil, because it's their fault I have suffered. The pain and suffering I feel every day is because of cruel people like him. I can't let this evil live on.

It's my duty to kill him.

It's my duty to avenge my friends and family. I know that now.

He places his forearm on my neck, choking me. I reach my arm over to my flame emitter and in less than a second. I aim at his face. Letting it emit flame. He blocked the full blast in his face, so it only hit the left side of his head. He rolls off me smacking himself in the face trying to put the fire out. Then finally removes his mask, revealing his identity.

The back of his head looks vaguely familiar, not including the half I lit on fire. I ignore it and silently walk closer to finish the kill.

"Well, I guess there's nothing I can do, just kill me bro." he turns his head slowly around facing mine, it takes a few seconds to render, but... it's him.

It's Ben.

His sad puppy dog eyes look at me with fear, betrayal, and even worse pain.

"Ben!" I fell to my knees, staring at his face. The face of a boy I remember, but not the same person.

"You murdered all of them, my friends, our friends," I yelled. That sadness I felt almost turned into anger and hatred for the boy that I wanted to avenge.

"No, not all but most, but I do have a reason for it." I can't even begin to think of anything that he could say that would justify his actions.

"I know what the reason is," I say staring into his eyes, intimidating him. "You joined them… the… the Russians. So, it's your fault my father is dead," I cry out, with a few tears running down my face.

"Hunter, my dad… he's alive." My eyes widen, and I drop my jaw. I don't even know what to think. Is this supposed to be a good thing? Ben's father wasn't exactly a role model, but Ben does love him.

"How? How is that possible?"

"When they blew up the beach, my father must have been out in the water or something. I'm told he has serious burns, and he will have a hard time functioning, but he will live. That is if I do what the Russians ask of me."

Shadow Venom

"How did you get drafted into the Russian military, and how do you know what they said is true?"

"When they breached land, they found my dad and checked his pockets, and they found his address in his wallet and snuck into my home and abducted me and my mother, so they told us the story and forced me to fight for them. So first I killed myself, so there wouldn't be any way for people to think it was me. Since my mother is an actress, she faked being sad about my death."

"But I saw your body," his body lay on my table, blood dripping from his neck. So full of life yet so lifeless at the same time.

"It was a fake, they make a replica," I've heard that people are taking other human bodies and giving them plastic surgery so they can trick others into believing they are dead.

"Dude, is my father alive?" My eyes become teary with hope, hoping my father is alive.

"No, I'm sorry." I fall to my back wondering what has happened, how is this fair. He murdered innocents, I murdered evil Russians, yet his father lives and not mine. "The night you first fought me, I wasn't coming to hurt you I was coming to warn you, but you ended up fighting me, and somehow winning, I couldn't kill you, you were my best friend." I stand back up wiping any dirt or dust off me then turning around to leave.

"Wait!" Ben calls, he chases after me but is unable to catch me. I ran back down to my motorcycle and started it up. I put one leg over the seat but before I can hop on a dagger is thrown at the seat behind me, it's Ben.

"Wait," he says glaring at me, trying to gain my attention and trust. "Please, I just want to help you. Even if my father dies. He had it coming to him from long ago, but we … we can still be friends." I look into his eyes, and he appears to be sincere, he isn't trying some sort of trick on me, so I decide to trust him.

"Okay, hop on, I'll take you back to the refuge building and you can meet Mark, but I can't guarantee he won't kill you on sight." I have a little trouble getting us going since it's a bigger motorcycle and I'm not used to extra weight, but we manage.

"So, are we good?" Ben asks me. I refused to respond for a few moments, but I eventually talked.

Shadow Venom

"Good is… is well not the word I would use, but I think I will trust you for now, but I will not hesitate to do what I need to, to stop the Russians."

"Understood, also by the way when I discovered you were Shadow Venom, I couldn't do anything to let harm come to you, so I helped you as best as I could, I couldn't do better."

"You're fine." once again not the word I would use, but what can I do? He saved my life. I do owe him that. I now must hope I can save his life, by making sure Mark doesn't immediately kill Ben on sight. Though he deserves it.

Part 3

"The Journey."

Shadow Venom

Jeremiah Anderson

Chapter 14

We approach the refuge building with caution, hoping no one will shoot Ben on sight. I handed Ben my mask and gave him directions to another entrance inside. I quickly change into civilian clothing and climb the wall briskly. When I reached the top, I jumped inside and ran for the entrance I told Ben about.

I dash down the hall hoping no one has caught Ben, but I'm too late, I see Ben in the custody of Mark. "Hey kid, this is no place for you."

"Never mind that now Mark, let Be… The Dark Condemner go. I have him under my watch." I nearly gave Ben's secret identity away, but thankfully I was able to stop myself before then. "He decided he was fighting for the wrong side, he's joining us."

"But he murdered innocents. Children!" Mark does have a point, but he's my best friend. He deserves a chance.

Shadow Venom

"I know, but please let him go." After explaining to Mark everything I know about Ben's situation with his father, he lets Ben go, but I made sure to use someone else's name. Instead of Bens. Which he doesn't need to know.

"He's under your watch though," Mark says. I thank Mark and proceed to show Ben around the place, from the roof of the building, since if anyone saw him, they probably would have had a heart attack and died.

"So, Ben, we need to take out some Russian bases, you up for the challenge."

"Am I ever," he says giving me a thumbs up and a nod of his head. We run to the edge of the building and jump off it to the ladder on the building across from ours and we slide down like butter in a frying pan. We hop on my father's motorcycle and head off to start our adventure.

~

When we reached the forest edge. I parked the motorcycle next to the bridge and almost fell into the river below with the weight of the motorcycle pulling me down.

"Whoa man, drowning isn't a fun way to die," Ben says laughingly.

175

Jeremiah Anderson

"Is there even a fun way to die?"

"I have no idea. I only know the painful ways." He stares into infinity blocking everything else out, I can see real fear in his eyes.

I figure I might as well help him feel a little less alone. "Same."

"Mm-hm," he acts as though he doesn't believe me. I can't help but wonder why. I pulled out my spare mask and we continued into the forest, hiking through the muddy ground. We collect berries along the way, so we don't get too hungry. I pull out a water filtration device that Ben and I both use to drink from. We both hunt for some small game, but neither of us catches anything, we walk along a river to hopefully find a base to destroy. The problem is with it still being day we will have to wait till nighttime anyway. Ben and I take pointy sticks and try to spearfish while we walk to keep us entertained. I stand alert ready to attack any Russian the moment I see them. I look at the sky and realize that even if I find a base, I will have a lot of time to kill, so I pull Ben over to the side and we build a raft to ride the river with, it should let our legs rest, and give us time to sit there and do nothing and maybe even get some rest.

Shadow Venom

When we finished constructing the raft, we put it on the river and carefully got on it without having it sink. It took a few hours to make, but it was well worth it. Water soaked through between the small gaps where the sticks could not fill.

I requested to take the first watch, Ben didn't hesitate to get some rest while I watched, he must completely trust me. I wish I felt the same way about him. Despite him being my best friend, he has still killed many innocents. Too many. It's like I'm looking at a complete stranger now.

I watch as the birds fly across the sky with such ease, without a care in the world, we are having war down here. They simply fly around and enjoy life, and at some point, die. I wish I was a bird. A snake slithers above the river in front of me, ignoring everything else other than its goal to get from one side of the river to the other, being a snake would be fun. I get to kill grown adults and I don't have to face the repercussions, because it's my nature. My eyelids become heavy. I can barely keep them up any longer, so I let them fall.

When I wake up, I see Ben taking a stick and paddling us along the river. He is watching the sides of the boat making sure that we aren't going too far under the water. We have been sinking. Only like three inches or so. Though

Jeremiah Anderson

Ben is so focused on the water he doesn't worry about me or whether I'm awake or not, or if I'm about to kill him without warning.

"Why hello, awake from your slumber I see," Ben says. Ben's face has a look of determination. He looks ahead of the river and points before I have the chance to look, he jumps into the water. I became very confused. I start to wonder if he has led me to a waterfall and has planned to kill me that way. But no, I look ahead, and it's a Russian base, I dive into the river before I can be spotted. I swam to the riverbank, surprised to see that Ben was coming to help me back up. I gladly accept his hand since I want to make amends too.

We walk along the water until we get a few yards from the base. We decided to climb the tallest tree we could nearby and camp out up there. "So, have you wondered what life would be like at this moment if none of this happened?" Ben randomly asks after having complete silence.

"No, not really," I reply quickly trying to forget. I'm not in the mood to chat. I try to focus on the Russians below. Ben continues to try to have a conversation with me, but I continue to shut him down. I can tell that he wants to have some fun, and I want that too. But I also want to stop the Russians from killing us.

Shadow Venom

When dusk arrives, we prepare ourselves to fight the Russians. "Okay Ben, you take left, I'll take right, sound good?"

"Sure thing," he said giving me this quick salute, and jumps into the next tree over and continues until fading into the darkness.

I climb down from my tree and sneak around into some bushes. I wait until a guard passes by next to the bush like he has been doing for the last few hours. The guard slowly marches through the thick grass, unaware of his future demise. I jump out of the bush and palm his gun away from me.

Before he could react, I sent my claws into his throat. Causing him to fall into the mud making a loud splat. None of the other guards appeared to notice, so I continued. I wonder how well Ben is doing, after all, his only competitions have been me and sleeping children.

I crept up to a campfire with three soldiers sitting around it. I shot my gun into each of their skulls and moved on. I reach my final campfire, so I try to enjoy it a little. I shoot two of the four guys, then sneaking up on one guy I hold his neck in my arm with a knife to his throat.

Jeremiah Anderson

The other guy fires into his buddy's chest thinking it will go through and hit me, but it doesn't. I dropped the dead body then kicked the other soldier's gun from his hand and stabbed my dagger into his heart.

I next headed to the main base to ignite the explosives. But before I did, I shot two soldiers patrolling the base and took their grenades. I unpin one and pull my arm back to throw it, but when I'm about to I see Ben running on top of the building taking guys out.

"Get down here, I need to blow this thing up," I try to whisper loudly, he ignores me and continues what he is doing. I look closer and notice that he isn't killing anyone, only shooting them in the legs or arms so they can't fight.

"Coming," he says leaping from the base and attempting to land properly, but he fails and crashes into the ground. I give a small laugh before remembering that I have a grenade in my hand and throwing it into the base, I help Ben up and we both run for the forest and duck for cover as the base blows. "Dude, you do that every night?" Ben asks, surprised that I managed to survive this.

"Yeah, not as easy as it looks huh?"

"No, but it was quite horrible. The evil and hatred in their eyes. Humans weren't made to do that."

"Why didn't you kill people?" I ask wondering why he refused to kill. "They aren't innocents, it's okay to kill them."

"Is it? Nobody needs to die; we can still win. Without causing the world to go up in flames."

What is that supposed to mean?

Of course, I need to kill people, they are not only evil but if they are only injured, they can be healed, then come back to kill me. "What are you talking about? The only way to win is to kill."

"We don't need to be as evil as they are. They haven't changed us as much as you think they did, we changed ourselves." Looking into Ben's eyes, I can tell that he isn't kidding, he means it. He doesn't want us to kill them.

"Do what you want, just don't get me killed in the process," I say walking away from Ben and heading to where I suspect the next base to be.

Jeremiah Anderson

Ben and I spent the last few days sitting in the trees and talking, and at night taking out bases, we managed to destroy fourteen, we are so close to being done. We crossed paths with Mark at one point and he told me how he had taken out three bases with his men, which means that there was one more base, the one that held me prisoner.

Ben and I walk through the forest, in search of the final base. Suddenly Ben falls to the ground. I duck down, looking around for any Russian soldiers around here who may have shot him. I don't see any soldiers around in the area, so I crawl over to Ben. I try to shake him awake, but he pushes me away, I search his body for any wounds, and I find nothing. He must have gotten too tired, so we took a break. I sit with my back against a tree keeping watch for any Russians that may pop up out of nowhere.

Getting tired of waiting I stand up and continue to walk through the forest a little further, I hear a bunch of men talking ahead of me, and my suspicions grow. I climb a tree, careful not to slip or make any noise. I get a better view of the area from up in the tree. I almost freeze in shock looking down, it's the base. The final one I need to take out. Briskly climbing down from the tree, I go to wake Ben. He lifts his head from the ground and shoves a bunch of grass under my mask.

Shadow Venom

"I'm sleeping, leave me be."

I consider just leaving him here, the Russians will discover him and kill him, he deserves it after everything he's done. But I can tell he didn't want to do it, so I'll try to give him the benefit of the doubt.

"Wake up, the Russians are here," I say as he jolts up from the ground and holds his daggers in his hands.

"Where are they, where are you?"

"Shut up, they're over there," pointing in the direction of the base, I cup my hand over his mouth and pull him to the ground. I don't need the Russians to discover that I'm on to them and have them take me out before I can even have the chance to fight. We both climbed to the top of a tree, Ben nearly fell from the tree. If he were to fall it would mean that immense attention would be brought upon us.

We would be captured and tortured beyond belief...

Dusk comes upon us, we climb down from the tree and head for the base, Ben goes left I go right. We both scale the massive walls that sit between us. When we reach the top, we stay close to the wall, so we don't get caught. Ben jumps onto a building and then slides down a pillar. I jump to a tree, but unable to gain a good grip I slip and fall to the ground. I can hear Ben chuckling at me, but when I turn my head, he stops laughing, acting as though he did nothing. I sent him a hand signal letting him know to move in. We both move in on opposite sides, so if one of us is caught, the other can continue to move in or save the other. A few guards walked past me, not noticing me in my hiding place. I shoot them all in the back and hurry over to their dead bodies to collect their ammo and grenades. Ben looks at me signing for me to hurry. I almost forgot, for years Ben and I have used sign language to communicate when we didn't want others to know what we were saying. We were able to do a lot of naughty things.

Forgetting that touching memory, I ran to hide inside of a jeep. I check to see if the coast is clear. When it is I climb onto a crate staying low, so I'm not caught. Ben runs straight across an open road, luckily, he is fast enough no one catches him. I jump from the crate landing on the ground with enough silence no one notices. I sneak across the road, without making a sound. Ben and I reunite on the other side to discuss the plan.

"Okay, so you have been able to wander around here with free will, right? Well, tell me where they keep the explosives."

Shadow Venom

"You know the crates that you have been jumping on?" I give him a couple of rapid nods showing him I understand and want to hurry this up. "Well, those are them. They are all over the base, but they space them equally apart so that if one were to go off it won't start a chain reaction."

I look to the ground trying to imagine a way we can blow this place up. I look up at the clock on the clock tower, and it takes a few seconds, but a plan hits me.

"I've got it, do you have timed bombs? Well let's use the clock to give us the time and we can set the time for the bombs to go off at midnight," I say eagerly.

Ben gives me a nod and hands me a key that he had in his pocket and points at the crates. I walk over to the crate while crouching and stick the key in the keyhole. I pull the door open, and I'm shocked to see almost every type of conceivable bomb in existence, but best of all. The timed bombs. I pick up a few and hand them to Ben. Then I placed one on the crate and set the timer for midnight. Ben stands straight up and gives me this salute. I guess it's time to get to work.

Jeremiah Anderson

I continue moving around the base placing the timed bombs on every crate I can find, setting each for twelve. Every few minutes I get bored, so I take out a few soldiers, for fun. Ben and I finally met back up after setting up more than thirty bombs. It's eleven forty-eight, so Ben and I decided it's time to get out of here. We try to sneak back the way we came, but when Ben steps out from behind the crate, a guard catches him. The Guard grabs his arm attempting to gain control of him, but Ben pulls out his dagger and stabs the guard in his hand. I shot the guard a couple of times, ending his life, and trying to help Ben. Many more men run at us, but we try to escape as fast as possible before we are killed. Ben and I climbed a building to reach the wall. We step a few feet back to get a running start, using all our strength we jump and smack into the wall, barely hanging on. I pull myself to the top and slide down the front of the wall to the outside. Ben stands at the top, pointing out into the distance. I see soldiers firing their guns at us, Ben shoots with his gun, and I move in and use my shield to block their bullets and slit their necks with my claws. I activate my electrified venom shocker and punch a couple of guys to get them to the ground before I jump on them and rip out their throats.

Shadow Venom

After I've seemingly gotten every soldier, I hear a gunshot to the left of me. I don't feel like moving, so I pull out my dagger and throw it at his head. Piercing the soldier's skull. I turn to look at Ben expecting him to be sliding down the wall to get out of here, but he stands there practically frozen. I turn my head to the side, confused as to why he isn't moving. I take a closer look and see blood flowing from his leg, he's been shot at least three times.

"Hurry," my throat choked, knowing that he could bleed out if I didn't get him to help.

"No," he refuses to move, he knows that he would weigh me down, it could get us both killed. I don't care, he's my best friend, he's coming with me. The gate slowly rises, and I can hear soldiers coming. If they come, Ben has no chance of getting out of here alive. Ben turns around to look at what I assume is a lot of soldiers, he turns to look at me and removes his mask. I shake my head, no. He lifts his chin, with a tear coming down his face. "Ben, No! Don't do it!"

"Go," he mouths to me. He fearlessly jumps down into a massive horde of Russian soldiers. I hear guns go off. It happens, the clock strikes twelve, and all the bombs go off. The walls to the base smash down into rubble, and

Jeremiah Anderson

I'm thrown back into the forest, the whole world seems to go by so fast. My mind can't focus, I'm dizzy, and I can't move.

Fear sets in, I've truly lost my best friend this time. It's all my fault, I could have saved him, but no. I stood there and did nothing.

Everything becomes black and fades away. As it did the day my father died.

Chapter 15

When I wake up, I can't see much, but I do see that I'm moving through the forest. I open and close my eyes until things become visible, once they do I look around trying to figure out where I am.

"You're awake. Finally. You can walk yourself," someone says. Eager to drop me. It takes me a couple of moments to recognize who it is that is holding me, but I soon realize that it's Ben. He bends down and throws me off his shoulders. I rolled down into a small puddle of water and hit my head on a rock. I don't even feel the pain with the tremendous happiness that I feel from seeing Ben again.

"Ben, you're alive," I yell. Jumping for joy knowing that I may have lost my best friend.

Jeremiah Anderson

Ben looks at me giving a smile before he continues to walk like I don't exist. I thrust myself up from the ground back onto my feet following Ben. "How did you live? I thought you died."

"How do you think I escaped before? There was a tunnel down there, and I needed to hold back the soldiers from killing you since the explosion was going to happen any second," Ben says taking a moment to catch his breath. "And if they escaped, you would have to fight them yourself. So, in conclusion, I shot half of them, while I was getting into my escape tunnel, then I found you and I've been carrying you ever since." Shame enters my mind, he has an injured leg and still carried me so far, and I've been considering killing him ever since I discovered his secret identity. "Ready to return home?" Ben asks, giving me a smile with one brow raised. I simply nod and we shift into a run.

We ran till we made it back to my father's motorcycle. When we got there, I told Ben to sit to the side while I got on the motorcycle. He doesn't question what I said. He obeys every request as an order. He's done so much for me. Including everything he did for me before this whole thing started. I don't even know how I can repay him, I guess the only thing I can do is not kill him. I help Ben onto the motorcycle, he nearly goes up on one side and then off the other, but I catch him before he falls. I hop on myself and start up the motorcycle. When I get it started, we ride down the road, feeling the nice breeze in the air. Morning is arriving so the air is nice and cool. The sky turns orange with the bright sun.

We rode up next to the warehouse and parked off to the side. I offer him help up a ladder, but he refuses it. When we get to the top, I help him inside through a hatch at the back of the building. He slides down the ladder with ease, until he slips and falls backward onto the ground, he cringes with pain.

"Shadow Venom, what are you doing here? You know you can use the front window as access," Mark says jumping out of nowhere, he doesn't seem to remember Ben's situation.

"But he can't, get him a medic please." I plead too Mark.

Mark gives me a nod and runs to get a medic; I hope whoever he picks won't want to kill Ben. I make sure Ben has his mask on in case whoever Mark brings won't recognize him and wants to hurt Ben. Mark returns with one of the most beautiful women of all time, my mother. She pulls down Ben's pant leg and begins to extract the bullets from his leg. Ben screams in agony, but I cover his mouth with my hand and hold him down so he can't do anything. He tries to fight back, but I'm stronger. I eventually have to push him onto his back and hold him down, so he can't fight back.

My mother moves on taking some chemicals and pouring them into his leg to clean it. The chemicals look unfamiliar, but if they can help Ben then so be it. When she finished cleaning the wound she wrapped a bandage around his leg, to stop any further bleeding. Mark picks Ben up and tries to carry him, Ben doesn't like it and places his hand around Mark's throat, but Mark ignores him and continues to carry him. Mark walks down the hall until he turns into a room, he turns into the cell that was previously holding a Russian soldier captive

"Why are you putting him in there? I thought we were going to pardon him."

"There's no room anywhere else," Mark says as I sigh in relief. I put my back against the wall and slid down it, waiting patiently for confirmation that Ben would be okay.

~

Shadow Venom

After a few hours of sleeping against the wall, I get up to check on Ben, but he's still asleep. A little later I go over to check on him again to set down a glass of water next to his bed and cover him in a blanket. I rest at his bedside until morning.

Mark bursts into the room with excitement, laughing with joy. Ben and I both wake up to see what the excitement is about. "Guess what guys, this is almost over, we just need to take out the ships on Long Beach and this will be over," Mark says gleefully shouting with joy.

Ben and I look at each other excited about the joy as well, but Ben's joy ends quickly. His eyes turn watery and become glassy. Every muscle in his body and face has weakened. Causing him to slouch over and become depressed looking. I wonder why for a few seconds, but it doesn't take long after that to figure out why. Even if we get through this, Ben would most likely be arrested or killed since he killed innocents, though he didn't have much of a choice. Being killed before the end of this might be a gift for him. Though he may get a quick death through legal punishment. There is no telling what people might do to him before then.

Jeremiah Anderson

"I will go tonight, alone," I say rising from the bedside. I tighten my fists and every muscle on my body as I walk to the door.

Ben grabs my hand and pulls me back before I can leave. "You're not going alone, I will come."

"No, you're in too much pain, and hurt too badly."

"Neither of you are going alone," Mark injects. "Both of you will not only be going during the day because at nighttime they will most likely take that opportunity to move back into the forest, but you will also have backup from me and the Strike Back Stingers." Mark pauses for a moment to look at Ben. "Also, Chad is coming. That's final." Ben looks over at me in confusion, wondering why he was called Chad. It was the fake name I gave Mark to protect Ben's identity. I placed my finger to my lip suggesting that he ignore it. Anyway, I wonder why Mark would even suggest Ben go, but he must suspect the same thing I do, that Ben will die a far worse death, than what could ever be given to him through combat.

He should die in the field.

Shadow Venom

Ben, Mark, and I along with some of Mark's men load up a few jeeps with equipment. Almost as soon as we finish, we jump in. Preparing to take out a fleet of ships.

Preparing to end this war.

~

We rode for over an hour in the vehicle before making it to Long Beach. We stop a half mile away and unload. We set up camp and a few tents with all the gear that Mark's men would need to survive. "Okay Men, gather up," Mark calls everybody together to discuss the plan, I see no point in having a plan, simply aim and shoot. But Mark prefers to be neat and organized. Regardless I say Mark lets Ben and I rush in and take the Russians out. "So, here's the plan boys. We need Shadow Venom and The Dark Condemner to oversee blowing up the ships, take those remote-controlled bombs and place them on each of the ships, then retreat. The rest of you will be with me and distract the Russians while they work. Troops fall in. Prepare for battle." After Mark explains the plan, he pulls Ben and me aside and explains the plan that he had prepared for us, but he can't tell the others since there may be traitors. Or maybe even spies.

Jeremiah Anderson

Mark acquaints us with a map he stole when he came to break me out of the Russian prison, but it's not a map of New York, it's a map of the west coast of Russia. Mark explains how he wants Ben and I to destroy every Russian ship we can and let one escape for us to ride on. He expects it to take us to Russia, where we will need to stop the Russians at the source. He can't come because he needs to stop any other Russian bases that could be forming. We are the best shot at finishing this war. Ben doesn't hesitate to accept the mission, knowing that there is no hope of a happy ending for him after what he's done.

Everybody moves in groups into the dense forest, Ben and I walk ahead of everyone so that if there is any surprise attack it happens to us first. When we make it to the edge of the forest, Ben and I go right and everyone else goes left. Ben and I ran as fast as we could to get to the farthest ship, there appeared to only be three, so we didn't have to run too incredibly far. There aren't that many so it shouldn't be too much trouble, right? Ben and I both carry large bombs in our bags, they weigh us down slightly, but we push through and act as though they aren't there. We ran across the beach, hiding behind crates and other military equipment. We wait for Mark and his men to start their fight, so we can attack. I take a good look at each ship and notice

196

that they are much larger than I had previously thought, but they don't look much like warships, more like big floating pieces of metal.

I hear gunfire off in the distance. Mark has begun his fight with his men. It's time for Ben and I to move in. We jump into the water and begin placing a few of the bombs under the ship. When we surface, we open the bottoms of our mask, so we don't drown. When we finish, we head to the top deck and place bombs above where the soldiers are, Ben uses both our shields to block their bullets while I place down the bombs. Once I'm finished, we move into the group of soldiers and finish them off. Ben continues to only cause injuries, but I follow up and go in for the kill. When we wrap up on ship number one, we jump into the water and swim to the next ship. We place each bomb accordingly, so when we activate them, the whole thing goes down into the water. I sign to Ben to start placing bombs on the top deck while I finish placing mine on the bottom deck.

When I finish, I swim to the surface to climb the ladder on the side of the ship. But when I peek my head over the edge of the ship, I pull it back down instantly, Ben is surrounded by some soldiers. I realize shouldn't have let him go alone. I pull out my gun and aim directly at a pipe, that I assume will release a toxic gas that will distract the soldiers, but also kill them. My hand is shaky, I can't tell why, I ignore it and fire my gun. The gas leaks everywhere, giving Ben the chance to escape. We are quick to place down every bomb we need to then run and jump from the ship. It doesn't take long for us to notice that the ships are pulling away from the beach, we swim with all our strength, but the current seems to not want us to make it to our escape ship.

When we reached the ship, Ben and I climbed a ladder and snuck around. Once we gain access inside, we look for a large vent to crawl into. I kick the vent open, bending the bars, but hopefully, no one will notice. The vent is dirty and dusty. Hardly a place I would like to spend my time. Ben and I crawl around and look around to try and find somewhere to access a window, we don't find a window, but we do find a vent leading outside. I kick it open and peek my head out.

I wait until it looks like Mark and his men are far enough away from us to press the button and blow up two of the three ships. When Mark is far enough away that he appears to be an ant. I press the button knowing that I am one step closer to winning. The bottom of the ships blows first, causing them to sink into the water, and the top blows next, killing every man on the top deck who hoped to escape the danger of sinking in the water. Ben and I remove our masks and sit in the vent watching the ships sink to the bottom of the ocean. Ben looks almost sorry for them, I consider asking why, but I don't think it will do any good right now. Ben probably has some personal reason for refusing to kill these evil men, but I don't, I will not stop.

If Ben and I can complete this final mission, everything will be over, I can go to the dance with Chloe, and everything can go back to normal... right?

Right?

Chapter 16

A couple of days have passed since we left Long Beach,

Ben and I grow hungrier by the minute. We can't wait much longer without food or water. We sneak through the vents until we reach the brig, at that point we try to stay out of sight until we can find some food compartment.

Ben and I decided to split up. It's dangerous but ensures finding food will be faster. I found a crowbar to open some crates with and discovered that they had hundreds of explosives on this ship, if this ship made it back safely to land, they could reload and my whole town, even America could be put at risk, even more than it already is. Before I leave this ship, I need to ensure that it blows up. I get tired from opening so many crates and nearly give up, but I open one more and it pays off, there's a whole crate with all sorts of food. I climb on top of the crates to try and find Ben, it takes a few minutes but when I do find him, I discover that he found food too. He sits there shoving as much food in his mouth as he can. I try to ignore his selfishness, but I can't help but give him a disapproving shake of my head.

We sit back and enjoy the food, until we become thirsty and need water. I put everything back so there is no sign of stowaways because the last thing we need is for people to discover we are here and come after us, we have no way to escape this place, so we need to be as sly as possible. We sneak around the ship, staying in blind spots that people won't see us in, and try to find somewhere to get water. Ben spots a water tank, so we head over to get some water, but when we do a soldier catches us, I quickly pull out my gun and aim for the skull. I pull the trigger. Ending our problem before we even have one. We continue before anyone else catches us. When we finish, we don't go back the way we came, we crawl into the nearest vent back to where we were hiding before.

We play games such as a game where you take your knife and balance it on your finger for as long as possible. We play without gloves on, which means the top of the knife goes directly into our fingertips. As the blade is being balanced on my finger blood bleeds out. It climbs down my index finger to my knuckles where it drips onto the cold ventilation metal. The weight of the blade feels almost as though it increases every second. Going deeper into my finger.

Ben at some point realizes it's too much for him. Causing him to throw the blade across the vent.

"Hey man, I'm getting bored, wanna chat?" Ben unexpectedly asks. I don't feel like talking. It's only that I'm afraid it could alert the Russians, but if I don't keep Ben busy. Knowing him. He might want to go and chat with our Russian friends.

"Sure," I say complying to talk with him, but I'm still cautious about the Russians.

"So, I was thinking, we have both forced change on ourselves so much, and I was wondering, we ourselves may not know how we've changed, so I was thinking that we take a minute and reflect on how everything has changed us." I take a minute to process what he said alone, then think about how I've changed, and I don't see how I've changed, not only that but if I have it's for the better. I explained that much to him, but he had this surprised look on his face like that was a complete lie.

Shadow Venom

"What, not changed? You have probably changed the most."

"Me? I'm not the one that's killed all my friends."

"No maybe you're not, but you're willingly slaughtering people, not afraid to cause pain or torture, this isn't the Hunter I knew. Haven't you ever hesitated to pull the trigger?" I think hard about what he said, and it almost makes sense, that must be why my hand was shaking when I was going to shoot the pipe with toxic gas to release on the soldiers to free Ben, but that was to save Ben. I couldn't save him without it, could I?

"I need to kill people, they need to die, they deserve to die for their crimes. They kill innocents, I kill guilty Russians who have taken everything from me," I say sitting up in defiance. I don't care about them or whatever family they have back in their homes, they deserve the death I have given them, worse even.

"Well, no one needs to die, and they didn't take everything, you did some of that yourself," Ben says crossing his arms in anger. Now it makes sense why he doesn't kill any of the Russian soldiers only injures them, he must be afraid of becoming one of them. Which he sort of already has. "Listen, I know I killed innocents. I thought I was doing the right thing. I was wrong. I don't want anybody else to die, that means both sides of this war. I just want people to stop dying," Ben says meaning every word. I understand what he says, it registers in my mind, but I ignore it, I want every Russian to be eliminated. "You don't need to feel such hate for the Russians, it's all just that they believe what they are doing is right, and it's okay for you to change, you just don't need to change into the evil that changed you." I ignore most of what he says because I know what mission I'm on and I will not rest until I've completed it. If I start being afraid to kill people, then I may not finish the mission and innocents will die because of me. Too many are depending on me to make the right choice. This is it.

Ben and I sat in silence for the next few hours, mad at each other disagreeing on what the outcome of this thing should be. I watch as the seagulls fly by the ship, and dive into the water. The birds fly into the water and fly right back out with a nice juicy fish, I wish I could get something tasty to eat.

When I was younger my father and I would go out into the ocean and vow to never return to land until we'd caught enough food to bring back to my mother. Almost every time we nearly starved ourselves. We had a water filtration device to get water, but other than that we only had fishing rods. We would get tugs all day until after a week or so we finally got lucky and got fish. But sometimes the fish would begin to spoil before we could get enough, so we would eat that and continue fishing. One time we spent almost a full month fishing until we caught enough food to bring back. My mother was not happy that we spent so much time, but my father had a couple of months off work and wanted to have a fun time with me. I'm not sure I enjoyed sitting and waiting for fish all the time, but I did enjoy the time spent with my father. I try to remind myself why I'm doing this, it's to avenge my father and to stop them from taking anything else away from me.

~

Ben and I spent another few days in the vents. I would go up every so often and get us a few cups of water to drink, and sneak us some food, but other than that we remained put. I try to get as much sleep in as possible, while Ben keeps watch, we often rotate between who sleeps and who stands guard in the possibility the ship turns around to go to America, or someone discovers us in the vents. I almost always find Ben asleep on the job, but I doubt someone will discover us here, so I don't mind it.

Jeremiah Anderson

After a couple of hours, Ben wakes up from sleeping on the job. I have a small chat with him to keep him entertained. I don't look at him, instead, I stare out of the vent of the ship and watch as ray-finned fish propel themselves out of the water at speeds up to thirty-five miles per hour. I've always found them interesting. They look as though they can fly. I would love to fly, but I'm not so sure I can build something capable of lifting me from the ground fast enough to escape my enemies.

Continuing the conversation with Ben, we discuss strategies to use to get into the Russian bases, and what we suspect them to look like. I know exactly what my plan is. Kill Russians, and don't let Russians kill me. It's simple, but it works.

The nights on the ship are cold. And when there's a storm it gets soaking wet. Ben and I tried to take the cold, but a few times Ben couldn't take much more of it and stole a blanket from the upper deck. I was asleep when he did this, but either way, I would not approve of it. Ben has offered to go get me one, but I don't want people to start noticing missing blankets, but if the cold gets too unbearable. I promised that I would go and get one.

When morning comes, I wake Ben and let him know that I would like to sleep, but he instead suggests that we go and get some food and that I'll sleep

Shadow Venom

better if we do so. Ben won't give this up, so I complied, and we head to the brig to get food. "Reminder, if we get caught, we could die. So, stay quiet," I remind Ben. He doesn't seem to worry much about getting caught, I don't think he fears death. I don't fear it, I just can't do it.

"Look you do still care for me. You can stop thinking I'm going to jump you," Ben says giving me a smug smile. He must have known what I've been thinking.   We crawl through the vents trying to get to the brig, but a few times we must be as silent as possible since we need to sneak past people on the other side of the vent. I break open the vent, and we crawl out of it. It's located not far from the entrance to reach the upper deck, but it should work, as long we are careful. The crates have been moved since the last time I was here, it has shifted into some labyrinth, I don't feel like puzzle games, so I climb on top to find the crate sooner. I searched my memory for any recollection of what the crate number was or what it looked like. I remember it having the numbers *2007*. I search from the top of the crates while Ben finds something to open them with.

Once I've located the crate, I look for Ben, but he's not in the room. I peek out of the door to the upper deck, and I spot him hiding behind a few

Russian soldiers. Ben steals a soldier's crowbar, causing the soldier to burst into anger, believing one of his comrades has taken it. The soldier freaks out beyond belief, he goes completely insane and pulls out a gun and points it at the other soldiers, telling them to give him his crowbar back. Ben looks like he's starting to panic, which he should be, so I use my gun to shoot the soldier in the back of the head. He falls forward and hits the ground. Ben gets shocked by it and jumps up. All the other soldiers ran around trying to grab their guns, Ben quickly pulled out his shield and ran back for the brig.

We can't go into the vents because then they could send a toxic gas in them to force us out, so we must hide in the labyrinth of crates. We continue to run until we reach a dead end. The soldiers aren't far behind, we try to climb the crate, but when I furtively look over the top, I notice that soldiers are at the top and are searching for us, the only way for us to escape is to either cause a distraction or to slow them down. Or kill every last one of them.

"We need to slow them down, any ideas?" I asked Ben.

"No, how about you?" Ben asks, unsure of what to do. I need to find a good distraction, and fast. The soldiers get closer as we speak, I notice a tank of water in the corner of the room. I could shoot their water supply, making

Shadow Venom

Shadow Venom

that their biggest issue, leading them away, or I could shoot the grenade on one of the soldiers' belts. killing them all ensuring they won't catch us.

I wanted revenge for my father.

I chose to shoot the grenade.

My hand shook uncontrollably. I refuse the other option, so I wrap my other hand around my wrist to get a straight shot. I carefully aim for the grenade because if I miss, they could figure out where I am.

This final mission is my last chance. My last chance to avenge my father and everything that he stood for. This is my last chance to prove to everyone that I will always be there for my family. No matter the cost. My last chance to heal the wounds the enemy gave me. If I lose. Then I will have failed my mission. My real mission is to protect my family. No matter what horrible things I have to do to protect them.

I pulled the trigger and let the bullet fly.

Right into the grenade, blowing everyone up.

I didn't think providently, the explosion also exploded half the supplies and food. I will focus on that later, but for now Ben and I sneak out of the brig and into the vent, we continue to crawl through it until we are sure we haven't been followed. I search for a few exit vents in case they track us down into the vents and try to use some sort of toxic gas to push us out or kill us.

After a few more days on the ship, being even more cautious, and not taking my eyes off Ben, we arrived. The land is in sight but not close enough to begin docking, Ben and I will use this as our chance to blow this thing up. I have no idea how we will return, but one step at a time. Ben and I climb out of the vents and look for a crate with explosives. We found one almost instantly since after I exploded a group of Russian soldiers, they thought that down here was haunted and would send only one man down there at a time, if the man was down here at the same time that I was present. I would kill him to keep their little suspicions up.

We load ourselves with as many explosives as possible and get ready to move throughout the ship, Ben takes the vents since he won't get in much trouble that way, and I will take everywhere else. I know the entire route in the vents by heart by now, so I will visit every vent and check if Ben has been there by peeking inside it. I carefully proceeded to gather my batch of explosives and move throughout the ship. I stealthily moved past the soldiers,

Shadow Venom

placing a few explosives right beneath them. I hide a few under some beds in their sleeping quarters and place some behind the edge of the ship.

When Ben and I finish we meet back up in the brig. We stuff bags full of food and water, since we don't know what we might get in Russia or when we will get it. We have about enough to last a week, maybe more. Both of us sneak up to the upper deck to exit, since we want to say goodbye to our hosts. We both climb up to the watch tower, a few guards try to shoot us, but I get them first. Once inside we figure out how to use it, and that's when the fun begins. I grab hold of the microphone and say my quick goodbye.

"Hello Russian rascals, how you are doing today? That's great because I have a very special surprise for you today, you are all going to die, enjoy," I say laughing maniacally to scare them. The crowd below screamed that there was a ghost, and I didn't pick the microphone up again to correct them. Ben and I slide down the ladder and find a good spot to jump ship. I found a small boat to make it to land on. I quickly lowered the boat into the water with Ben in it, then I used a rope to lower myself in.

Ben rows the boat for the first little bit, then I take over and we continue until we have made it a good distance away from the ship. I pull out the detonator and look up at Ben almost asking his permission to press it, he gives me a simple nod, so I press it. The entire ship blows, it looks like fireworks, the missiles inside the ship blast out of the ship into the water and blow up creating this awesome water and light show. After succeeding in blowing the ship I focus my attention on the mission, When I finally take a moment to look at Russia, I notice it looks like a snow globe had thrown up on it, the place is covered in snow. This mission might be harder than I thought. I gather my senseless thoughts and continue to row to land.

When the boat hits the sand along the beach, we climb out of the boat and search for a place to put it in case we need to use it as an escape boat. I carry most of the items since Ben is having a hard time walking with his leg. Snow isn't falling now, but even without it, the air feels like I'm stuck in a freezer. I look for signs of life, but I don't see many man-made objects.

We hiked through the forest in search of shelter, it took a few hours, but I eventually found something that might work. I found an old cabin with furniture, cooking supplies, and some matches for a fire. I went outside to try and find some dry wood. It took a while, but in due course, I found some. I start up a fire to keep us warm. Ben grabs a blanket and removes his clothes to warm up as much as possible, I do the same, and we both hang them over the fire so when we need them, they will be nice and warm. Ben and I barricaded the door so no one could get in. I tried to stay awake and keep watch, but I wound up getting too tired and slowly drifted away next to the fire.

Chapter 17

I wake up to the early sun and start up breakfast for Ben and me. The food isn't the best, but it fills us up and that's all that matters. I built another fire since the last one went out in the night, everything in the room feels cold to touch. I found a few candle lanterns that I use to light things up around the place more. Now that I get the chance to, I look around and see that this cabin is larger than I thought, it has two bedrooms, and a kitchen, and the main living room is quite large as well. Ben gets up on his feet and grabs his blanket to wrap around his waist since our clothes are still drying. I do the same since I don't need to go around naked. Ben sits at the table and eats his breakfast. He doesn't talk much, nothing more than a few grunts. I don't worry about it since I have bigger issues, like dealing with Russian bases.

I tried to visually remember Mark's map, but I didn't get that long of a look at it, maybe a couple of seconds of it, but we had to hurry. Ben and I

Shadow Venom

gear up and get ready to head out into the field and slaughter some Russians. I will take some matches and a lantern with me just in case we need them. I will need to be cautious so that I don't get caught if I start a fire. The smoke could float up above the trees alerting everyone of my location.

We hike through the forest for a couple of hours before taking a small break. The cold seeps into our bones. Every muscle on my body can hardly move. The cold bites my fingertips until they become a bright shining red which is a clear indication of frostbite. I didn't think that it would be this cold in Russia, I figured it would be cold. But not this cold. This is worse than New York.

"Dude, I feel like I'm going to die, I can't do this," Ben cries.

"Keep it together. We just need to survive long enough to take out a few Russian bases, once we have completed the mission we can head back and get a nice hot cup of cocoa and sit by the fire," I say trying to comfort Ben, but he doesn't care. I continue anyway, but don't get anywhere, so at some point, I stop.

Jeremiah Anderson

We continued hiking through the snow. I soon find that it gets deeper as we continue, so I find a few tough pieces of bark, and I use some rope and tie them to Bens and my feet. Now we don't have to worry about falling into the snow. The snow blows harder, which seems to be a good thing and a bad thing. It will cover our footprints so we can't be followed, but it will also make this a colder and much more painful hike. The cold bites into my skin, feeling almost like the stings the wasps gave me when I had to fight in the stadium. My blood turns cold like it did when I was in that life-or-death situation against Adrick.

I try to not think about it, but it continues to enter my mind. Dodging the attacks of the man who nearly killed me. Adrick Kim. I remember everything so vividly, it's almost as though it's happening right now. I fear the possibility that he will return.

I mean Ben, someone who I thought was dead has returned. What would I do if Adrick came back to kill me? For all I know he gained immunity to death. Maybe everyone has and I don't know it. I don't know what I would do if I were to be captured by Adrick Kim and forced to face him again. The only reason I won was because Ben kicked that spear into the stadium, I wouldn't have won otherwise. I look at Ben, watching as he walks through the snow, struggling with his leg. I haven't even given his leg much thought. I want to protect those I care about, and I haven't even been able to focus on the one that's right next to me. I walk over to a tree and look for a dead stick. I look until I find one suitable for walking with, I hand it over to Ben, so he can take some weight from his leg. He refuses it, but I carry it anyway since he might want it later.

Ben places his hand on his stomach, indicating he's hungry. I look for something to eat, but I don't know the Russian wilderness very well, so I don't take any berries to eat since I don't want to be poisoned.

I get bored of the silence, so even with snow barely falling I decide to try and start up a conversation with Ben. "So, what are your plans when all this is over?"

"Assuming that I don't go to prison for my actions. I would want to try to get things back on track, if my father makes it out alive from the Russian's capture then I want to live life to its fullest." Hearing Ben say that weighs a heavy weight on my heart, I know that in the end, Ben will not have a happy ending, it's either death or prison or prison till death.

Jeremiah Anderson

"Just have hope. I hope that everything works out," I say, Ben turns his head towards me and looks as though he wants to reply but doesn't.

The snow cools down, things seem to get better until I notice something in the snow. I walk closer to it cautiously hoping to get a better look, but that's when I see that it's tracks, polar bear tracks. I've always loved bears in general, but I've always feared polar bears. I know how to survive black bears and grizzlies, but with polar bears, there's little to no survival. I keep a keen eye out for any bears that could attack Ben or me, but I should be safe if I make sure there aren't any around us, and if one pops up, then that's the end of the line for me. Seeing as the snow cooled down, Ben and I took advantage of the opportunity to mess around a little.

We also need to make noise, so any bears around the area will know that we are here and not be taken by surprise. "It's always better to alert the bear, than become a small appetizer," as my father used to say. I probably wouldn't even be able to do what I'm doing today if it weren't for my father, he taught me almost everything there is to know about the forest, one thing he neglected to teach me is what to do when you're stuck in Russia and need to take out entire bases of Russians.

Shadow Venom

Ben runs over to a fallen tree and pulls off a few branches, they are both long and dried. He throws one at me and I gladly accept. I hold the walking stick I found, and the stick Ben tosses over to me. Ben holds two sticks as well. Ben charges right at me with both sticks and tries to hit me with them. I dodged with ease; I returned the attack by sweeping him off his feet. Ben regains his footage and holds both sticks low on the ground, in some sort of battle stance.

"You know, we're just messing around, no one needs to die," Ben says, giving a loud laugh. I haven't heard a genuine laugh from him in a while. It's nice to have fun and fight someone without needing to kill them. Ben and I gradually move in the same direction as we were before, slower but time goes by quickly since our minds are both occupied with having fun.

Ben trips me onto my feet. I expect him to attack me, but he doesn't, instead he runs up a hill. I figure it might be a good vantage point since we need to start focusing on the mission. Ben climbs a bit further up the hill, before stopping to look back down at me, he waves down at me trying to show me how high he is. Suddenly something feels wrong when Ben looks over his shoulder and screams, he leaps down the hill rolling in the snow, and sinking in it. He doesn't stop at me, instead runs right past me. I attempted to take a closer look. I don't see anything and almost believe he is playing a prank on me. Snow rolls down the hill down to my feet, I look back up again to see what he screamed about, but as I look closer my heart beats louder and louder until I hear Ben scream again from behind me.

"Run!" I can't figure out why he would be telling me to run, so I look closer, and a giant figure emerges from behind a large tree, a moose. I turn around and run for my life, if there is anything I fear more than a bear, it's a moose. A bear might slaughter me, but a moose with crush me to death. I would still probably rather the moose over a polar bear, but either way wildlife isn't fun to deal with unless I'm eating it. I ran and hid behind a tree, the moose was only seconds behind me, it charged right past me and continued to run. I look ahead of the moose and the tree it heads for; the same one Ben is trying to climb. Ben barely makes it above the moose's head level when it rams into a tree, Ben falls into a pile of snow cushioning his fall, but the moose prevails for Ben.

The moose gets ready to crush Ben when I pull out my gun and fire at it, the moose takes the hits and turns to me. He locks eyes with me and charges for me. I don't stop firing at it, but my hand continues to shake rapidly. I try to grab my hand to steady my aim. But I can't.

The moose is seconds away from hitting me. I try to jump out of the way of its charge, but it clips my shoulder just as I jump. Causing my arm to have extreme agonizing pain. I land in a pile of snow, but I sink into it. I can't get out of it, it's like quicksand, causing me to be helpless to the charging moose. Seeing nothing more than a moose charging at me between the snow piles around me, I figure this is it, and I pray it will be fast.

The moose looks at me with evil angry eyes. Almost the same eyes Adrick looked at me with.

When the moose is only a few yards off it steers off course. I wonder why it would stop when I was right in the line of sight to be killed, but moments later I see Ben walking towards it blasting full flame of his flame emitter towards the moose, it appears to have run off being afraid of the fire.

Ben walks over to me and offers me a hand, I don't want to give him the impression that I can't help myself, so I try to dig out of the snow myself. I struggle to get out and wind up having to hold my hand out for Ben to pull up.

"Well, that was fun," Ben says gleefully, I turn to him and pull off my mask dropping my jaw and widening my eyes in awe. He laughs with jubilation, giving me a pat on the back and pulling me in close as we walk through the forest.

I consider killing him now, but he did save my life.

I keep an extra keen eye out for moose since I have now developed a fear of moose. Ben and I walk through thick underbrush and high bushes, thorns consistently get caught on my suit, so I must use my dagger to cut away at plants in front of me.

Ben runs in front of me to stand on the mound of snow, I don't think much of it. But when I look down, I see something sticking out, something that looks like it has claws. I stare at it for a couple of seconds before fear sets in.

"Ben, get over here now," I say as gently as possible, he slowly walks back over to me, without question. The mound of snow rises from the ground with snow falling around it, revealing itself to be a massive polar bear. "Run," I can barely whisper to Ben. We both turn around running through where we came from for someplace with protection, but the bear runs close behind us. I wouldn't run from any other bear, instead, I would do the appropriate thing for its type, but polar.

I'm running for my life.

We find this log that appears to be big and thick enough to give us protection, I let Ben enter first since I want to keep track of the bear's location. When Ben is fully inside, I enter myself.

I watch as the bear runs over to the entrance of the log, it tries to reach through the opening, but I have concealed myself far enough that it can't reach in and grab me. The bear calms down and walks away appearing to get tired and realize we are not worth its gruesome time. Crawling further forward I still hear nor see any sign of the bear still being here, so I get ready to let Ben know that it's safe to exit when the middle of the log smashes down. I look back and the bear has used its mass to crush the log like a grape. Ben is in the grasp of the bear's claws. I quickly pulled out my gun and fired every shot I could at the bear. I'm not thinking straight and don't realize that I should be shooting the bear's head not to body, but not before it charges at me.

I pull out my katana and swipe it in front of me keeping distance between the bear and me. We circle the bear as it tries to go around the katana, but I make sure to keep that distance. I notice Ben is trying to stand back up after being hit by the bear. I try to keep its attention on me, but Ben sees me with the bear, confused and dizzy, he runs at the bear holding a dagger in his hand. The bear is too focused on me to notice, so I keep his attention on me. Until Ben jumps onto the bear's back and repeatably stabs it in the neck and back. The bear tries to fight him, but it doesn't live for long after I slice my katana into its throat.

Ben falls to the ground in pain. I run to help him and find injuries, but I don't see anything that looks like it would be severe enough to kill him. Nothing more than a few scratches. Ben looks towards a patch of bushes. I can't tell why, but he walks over to them, sticks his hand in it, and pulls out a few berries. My face lights up with excitement, as I start to reach for the berries in his hand, but I refuse and let Ben eat them. I recognize the berries, so I know they are safe. Ben pulls off his mask gobbling the berries in seconds. I wait for Ben to finish grabbing as many berries as he wants before

Shadow Venom

I move in myself. If Ben hadn't found that bush, we might have starved to death. Since the cabin is so far back, it would take hours to return to it.

Suddenly I hear ruffling in the bushes, I squint my eyes to get a better look, I'm shocked when the moose returns running out of the bush and ramming its powerful antlers into Ben, throwing him into the ice-capped lake I hadn't noticed before.

The impact of Ben hitting the lake causes him to break the ice and fall into the icy cold water. The current pulls Ben even more under the ice.

If I don't act fast, Ben will die.

Chapter 18

Rushing down to the river, I look for a way to break the ice.

My breath is heavy, and I fear for the life of my best friend. I can't let this be it. This isn't the end. I will save him.

Ben grips onto the ice with his claws and looks to be holding on well, but if I don't hurry there are several ways he could die, hypothermia, lack of oxygen, or some deadly creature in the water. I found a thick stick that appeared to be strong enough to break the ice. I lift it high above my head and slam it into the ice, it barely causes a few cracks. So, I tried again and again and again. I continue to bang on the ice. My breath grows short, I stop to look at the ice, but I don't see much improvement. Any longer Bens not going to make it. I stop for a few seconds to think of a way to break the ice, without realizing it I lift my right arm and blast the ice with my flame emitter. I try to keep it going as long as I can, but the flame becomes weaker and weaker until it goes out.

Quickly reloading the cartridge, I blast another full cartridge of butane onto the ice, it melts fast, but not fast enough. One of Ben's hands has already become too weak to hold on, so it lets go and waves freely in the water. I can see Ben's other hand is slipping. When the ice thinned enough, I stomped on it with all my might. The ice breaks and allows me to reach in and grab Ben, when I touch the ice, it is so could I almost pull my hand out, but Ben's entire body is in there and freezing him to death, so I continue. Ben is so far in that I plunge my whole body in to grab him. I pulled him on the ice hoping to save him. He appears to be breathing heavy breaths. His skin is like touching a piece of ice.

I drag Ben back onto land and lay him down in a pile of snow. I cover him with snow to conserve any body heat he may have left. I pick up a few dry sticks and place them in a pile. I use my flame emitter to start a fire. The sticks go up in flame almost instantly. I pulled Ben out of the snow and laid him down next to the fire. I let him try to heat back up while I sit there and relax, hoping Ben won't die.

When night approaches, Ben wakes and sits up. He looks all over his body, surprised he is alive. He crawls closer to the fire practically touching it. I figure since there is so much snow around, he could instantly put out the fire if it was caught on him if he needs to. I stared at the side of his face where I used my flame emitter to burn half his head a little while ago, if he hadn't moved in time, it could've been to whole thing. He still has plenty of bruises and cuts from when I tried to beat the life out of him. It pains me to know that I had the strength to do something like that to him.

"Thank you… for… saving my life," Ben still looks a little low on air, but he should be fine.

"You're welcome," I say. "Think you'll be, okay?" I ask eagerly.

"Yeah, I should be fine, though there is something I've been meaning to ask you…" He wants to start a conversation when he should be focused on breathing. Long as he's fine it doesn't matter. "You've become this killing machine, you act as though you only want death," Ben says looking up at me.

Shadow Venom

"Why?" How could he dare ask something like that after I saved his life, he's not wrong but still.

"You're right the attack of the Russians has changed me. They have changed me. But for the better," I say in the hope of defusing the conversation. But in reality, I'm only escalating it.

"Why did you name yourself Shadow Venom?" Ben asks. Looking me in the eye, demanding an answer from me, but I almost refuse to answer until I succumb to his staring.

"Because… after the attack, I knew I needed to change. So, I wanted to become someone who can finish this thing and get it over with," I say. "Someone that can protect those he cares about when they are in danger. I wanted to change into someone who is to be known as a beacon of fear and death, anything that would make people fear me enough to end this," I say as I rise from my seat and look to the stars.

I shift my head over to Ben. "Shadow. People fear the darkness because they don't trust what they don't know, and you don't always know what lurks in the darkness," I say. "Venom. People fear creatures such as snakes, wasps, spiders, and numerous other creatures with venom in them," I say staring endlessly at the stares. Trying to act as though I can justify the lives I have taken. "When they entered my life, they scared me, so I have become the very thing they would fear."

Ben looks me in the eye, frowning with what he heard. "Have you hurt anybody?" Ben asks as his voice shakes with slight fear.

"Of course, I have, how do you expect me to win this thing?"

Anger enters Ben's eyes, as he rises from the ground to stand level to me "That's not what I meant."

"Uh," I say as my voice cracks. "When I went to my self-defense class, everything went blank and I was fighting a Russian soldier, but when I woke. I found Gideon Yael on the ground, bleeding. I hurt him," I say rushing to get it over with. I do feel guilty about it but, in the end. I'm doing the right thing. Certainly. Absolutely. Maybe?

"Because even though you act like you're fearless, you fear a lot, that's why you had a flashback," Ben says, trying to figure out what to say next. "It's okay to change Hunter, but you don't need to become the evil that changed you."

Shadow Venom

I roll my eyes at Ben, showing my displeasure. "You already told me that," I say turning around to walk away.

Ben grabs my arm, stopping me from moving away. "Yeah... well maybe it's something that you need to hear." I pull my arm from Ben's grasp and continue walking away from him until I think I've gained enough distance that he won't see me. I pull out my dagger and give a loud grunt while stabbing it into a tree. I plop into a pile of snow and watch as the stars sparkle in the night light.

How could Ben say that to me? I changed because I wanted to overpower the Russians. I want to be someone who can win this war and finish it. How could he not understand that?

I soon got up and wandered around in the forest for a few minutes, I tried to be more cautious than Ben was when he got a moose and a bear to chase us. Plus, this time, I won't have to worry about Ben since I'm on my own. As I hike up the side of the large hill, I find that the moose is waiting on a ledge. It huffs and puffs at me, but before it can attack, I send five bullets into its skull. It makes a loud moan as it falls down the side of the hill. I can't help shooting it one more time before turning around and continuing my hike. The top of the hill gives me a perfect view of the surrounding forest. It's even colder up at the top with it being a tall hill. I notice bright lights in the distance. I lean forward with curiosity. I realize it must be one of the Russian bases. I might be able to take them out tonight. I look a little further, and I see a second base.

My body shifts from feeling tense to being completely relaxed. I figure since there are only two bases from what I can see now it shouldn't be too difficult to infiltrate. The mountainous terrain around this area makes it hard to get a good view of the whole area, I only hope that those are the only two there are and that I won't have to deal with what I had to in New York, getting captured and tortured.

I found a hollow log, so I dragged it over to a less steep slope for me to ride down. I push it a little off the edge, giving it a running start, I then jump in and enjoy the ride. I sit back and relax on the slope down, feeling the fresh air coursing through my hair, and the fresh pine smell in my nose. The ride comes to a halt when a tree too large to swerve around is in front of me. I quickly jump out of the log and land in the snow, it gets in my eyes nose, and mouth. I don't complain since when the log hit the tree it shattered like glass.

Shadow Venom

After picking myself up from the ground. I hiked back to Ben to let him in on the news that we might be able to get back home sooner. Once this mission is complete, we can finally go home and get our lives back on track, or at least I can. When I reached the campfire, I found Ben fast asleep curled up next to a tree. I sit down next to the campfire since with Ben asleep I will need to be the one to keep watch all night. I don't mind since I can operate well not getting much sleep, Ben on the other hand. He certainly needs sleep.

When we were younger, Ben and I decided that we would go out into the woods and see how long we could go without sleeping. I figured I would win but Ben was insisting he would, so I decided to create the challenge. We spent about twenty-eight hours in the woods before Ben started falling asleep while lying in a tree, he fell a good twenty feet before hitting the ground and breaking his shoulder. I rushed him back home so we could call the ambulance. I rode the whole way to the hospital by his side, he never spoke about the challenge again, we both tried to forget it since his father wasn't happy. I think that might be one of the reasons his father doesn't like me.

~

Jeremiah Anderson

I wake up and I'm back in the forests of New York. Adrick is running for me. I look behind me to see if I have a clear path to run, but I do not; the forest that surrounds me is covered by thorn bushes, and the trees have unnatural spikes coming out of them. I pull out my gun to shoot Adrick, but when I pull the trigger, nothing comes out, my magazine is empty. I lift my arm to use my flame emitter to roast him alive, but it's jammed nothing comes out. My electrified venom shocker breaks away on my arm and rusts away into the gentle breeze. Adrick moves closer and closer by the second. I reach behind my back for my shield, but it isn't there, nor are my daggers or katana. I panic as he gets closer. I lift a stick from the ground to throw at him but he's invincible, he smashes every tree he comes across, and the chips of wood fly everywhere.

Bracing myself for the impact, I turn my head while placing my arms over my chest to protect any vital organs. But with his strength, he would destroy me. I don't run since I couldn't outrun him if I tried. Adrick grabs a tree with his bare hands and lifts it above his head, throwing it to the ground and smashing it into trillions of pieces. The shards of wood fly at me, cutting my arms, they don't seem to hurt. I figure the adrenaline must be preventing me from feeling it. I block as many as I can by covering my face with my arms.

Shadow Venom

Once I look between my arms, Adrick stands there in front of me, looking down upon me like some rodent he caught in a trap. Which he did since I have no escape. I close my eyes gently hoping it will be quick, but he grabs my throat and lifts me against a tree, the spikes stab into my back, but still no pain.

Blood dripping from Adrick's chest, from where I stabbed him. I almost consider apologizing, but that wouldn't be nearly enough.

He looks at me with those evil eyes. "Wake up!" Wake up? What does he mean? "Wake up! Hunter!" How does he know my name?

A bright light shines in my eyes, I can't tell where is coming from since the trees are blocking most of the light.

"Wake up!" The voice changes, it's Bens! "Wake up!" My eyes fly open. I burst out of my snow bed. I find Ben shocked with worry in his eyes. I don't speak, I merely look into Ben's eyes until he decides to talk. "What's wrong man?" Ben asks. "Are you okay? What happened?"

"I... don't know," everything around me appears dizzy, I start to lay back down but Ben catches me and tries to help me focus. I watch as he picks up this tree bark bowl and gets some water from the river. He walks back over to me and kneels. I expect him to hand it to me to give me something to drink, but instead, he splashes it in my face.

The cold water drips down my face and into my clothing. I "What was that for?" I say as I stand up in anger.

Ben's eyes are full of laughter and joy, but he tries to keep calm. "You were sweating and talking in your sleep, something about Adrick."

I figured that I couldn't keep it secret forever, so I went on to explain what happened. Ben didn't look shocked, he looked more like this was the second stage of me going crazy. If so, he might be right. Ben and I clean things up in our little camping spot, so people don't discover us here, while I explain where I saw the Russian Base. He mostly nods instead of engaging in the conversation. I think he's thinking about my dream since he appears to have expected this.

We head in the direction of the bases as Ben, and I silently walk through the snow. When we reached the river, I walked across it without worry, but when I turned to look at Ben, he stood off to the side of it, afraid to enter. I locked his eyes with mine reassuring him that if something happens, I will save him. He steps onto the ice carefully as though it's made of glass, but considering how long it took me to break it, I know it isn't nearly as fragile as he treats it. The both of us continue to go in the direction of the bases until we reach a small hill across from them. When I take a closer look, I feel as though I'm seeing triple, because in the middle there's a larger base, larger than any of the others, it's like an entire facility. It looks like it would be too big to destroy.

What am I going to do?

Chapter 19

Ben looks at me almost as though he thinks I lied to him, though I thought I only saw two. I notice a mountain surrounding the third base. It must have concealed it from my sight.

"I thought you said two bases," Ben says with an angry tone.

"With all the mountainous terrain around here, it must have blocked my view."

"That isn't even a base," Ben says with a rising tone. "That's a facility, a prison. Or anything else you can think of that's really big." He's right, it's larger than any other Russian base I've ever been to. We both decided to wait until nightfall to attack. I make a small bed out of some pine needles, while Ben gathers wood for a fire. I stand the wood up to form a small teepee, then set the wood on fire with a match. Ben and I sit around the fire waiting for the night to come. We both try to get as much rest as possible before attacking the bases.

I'm too afraid to sleep.

I stayed up the entire time, listening to the birds chirping and the large gusts of cold wind flowing through the trees. I spent most of the time wondering what my dream meant. Is this a sign? Is he coming back for me? What if I lost so much blood that I only imagined that I killed him in the end?

It has become dusk. Ben and I clean up our camping spot and prepare to move in to attack.

We hide behind trees and other large obstructions of their view, so the moonlight doesn't give us away. We decided to go for one of the two small bases first. I notice they don't have campfires around them like they do in New York, then again, this place looks like it would freeze fire. I walk through the snow up to the base with Ben trailing right behind me. I found a nice tall tree that will get me over the wall, but I don't know how I will get out. I climb regardless of not having a plan, the view from the top is spectacular.

Jeremiah Anderson

The freezing wind bites the exposed skin on my body from where my suit was cut. My goggles begin to become covered in the frost of the air. It becomes difficult to see. Though I have enough strength and confidence right now to take down this place blind.

I skillfully climb along the branch overhanging the wall. Ben struggles on the slippery bark, but he continues anyway. We hang from the branch by our hands, then when it becomes too much we drop down to the top of the wall without a sound.

We crawl around the wall until we reach a guard tower. I pulled out my gun. And I shot everyone in the tower and climbed to the top. I access the controls to open the front gate so Ben and I can escape. We look around for someplace that might contain explosives. I almost consider moving on without explosives until Ben locates a missile silo. Now I need a way to get there without getting killed. I take the fire hose off the wall and throw it over the side of the tower, Ben, and I slide down it easily without any problem. We ran behind a bunch of crates that I can't help but wonder if they might be filled with explosives. I open a few using a crowbar, but they only contain stuff like blankets and food. Ben reaches into a crate for food, but I slap his wrist letting him know this isn't the time.

Shadow Venom

We've made it around the base. It took a good amount of time but it's probably the easy part of this. I open a door to the missile silo, but nothing is in it. Not a single explosive. I hear men running up to the door, screaming in Russian. Ben and I rush to climb a ladder to gain higher ground. The men burst into the silo, shooting their guns everywhere they can. Hoping to land a bullet on their most deadly enemy... and Ben. But they don't get a single drop of blood from us. Ben and I continue to run, but we come to a dead end and right when it looks like they've got us, they retreat from the silo. I'm curious as to why they don't pursue us, so I climb another ladder to a balcony outside the silo. Looking off in the distance I can see the men load themselves up in jeeps and ride off. I assume they got scared and ran off, but I don't see anyone else in the base anymore. However, I do see vehicles riding off through the forest.

Ben and I climbed down the ladder and headed into the heart of the base. I find this tall building with a symbol on top, but I can't make it out in the night light. I walk into the building with my shield and gun ready to kill. I discover that no one is here, the place is abandoned. I walk around for a few minutes until I find a room that looks like a fancy office. I enter the room and find a book on the desk. I picked it up to read it, but I'm unable to read Russian. Ben finds a translator book that he uses to translate the words on the front of the book.

Ben's eyes widen with shock. "It says... Soviet... Soviet Union Negotiations," Ben says with fear. "What is this?" Ben tears his mask off his face revealing his face to be completely white with fear.

"I don't know," I tell Ben trying to calm him down. I don't understand myself. The Soviet Union couldn't start a war with the United States because it could result in a nuclear war. But they were certainly hiding something. Ben continues to translate the rest of the book, but he doesn't find anything else of importance in it other than the dates ships have been sent to America.

When we get ready to move on to the next base. I notice Ben carries the book with him in his hand. I guess he thinks it will come into use later. I don't, so I swipe it from his hand, walk over to a hollow log, and place it in there. "You need both hands to fight, you can have your toy later," I tell Ben. If Ben isn't going to go for the kill. He can't be holding onto anything that may prevent him from using self-defense.

Shadow Venom

When we reached the second of the three bases, Ben noticed a ladder to get over the wall. I feel concerned about why they have a ladder on this side of the wall since the purpose is to keep people out. But I climbed it anyway. When I make it to the top, I jump onto a nearby building's roof, then I slide down the roof landing on the concrete roof. Ben jumps after me having a surprisingly nice landing. We tread lightly along the roof, making sure the soldiers below don't see us. Ben walks closely behind me. But getting distracted I trip on a small escalation of the building, causing me to fall off it. Behind a bush.

My fall was loud, too loud. The soldiers turn and start firing into the bush. I was fast enough to grab my shield so that their bullets didn't harm me. I can hear and feel that they have changed the direction of their aim and are now shooting at Ben. Thankfully it didn't take long for the firing to stop. But I know that Ben still has refused to kill them because I can hear groaning, not dead silence. I stand back up with my gun in hand ready to shoot anyone who dares to mess with me. I see the men lying on the ground in pain, I consider shooting them. But instead, I drag them behind a bush, so they can suffer in pain. Ben looks at me and shakes his head slowly from side to side in disappointment. I disregard it and move on.

Climbing up a pillar to get back on the roof I ran across the rooftops until I found the end. Ben and I overlook the area and find someplace that could hold explosives. Both of us climb down from the building and sneak behind a group of soldiers in front of us. They look like they are watching some speech in the other direction. The soldiers appear to be preoccupied with watching the speech, so I shouldn't have to worry about them.

When the soldiers suddenly stop talking, my heart pounds against my chest like it wants to break out. The soldiers turned to look at Ben and me. They all rise and cock their guns. Preparing to fire. A soldier yells something at the top of his lungs in Russian, causing all the others to fire at Ben and I. Luckily; we were both smart enough to pull out our shields to protect ourselves from the bullets. I pull out my gun, as Ben does his, and we fire at the group of soldiers. I aim for the head, so I don't need to shoot them twice, while Ben shoots the legs. They begin surrounding Ben and me, we move back-to-back, and we shoot every soldier that comes near us.

The soldiers move in closer as Ben and I become more and more trapped. "I want you to know if this is it. You were always my best friend, other than the time you took Chloe to the dance. I hated you then," Ben shouts as he is drowned out in the loud sound of gunfire from the other soldiers. A few bullets graze my skin, and the blood from my arms and legs drips down into my boots and gloves.

"As are you, my friend." I don't go for a deep emotional goodbye since I believe we will make it out of this. I look around for a possible way to escape, but there is no direction we can run without getting shot. I look down at my belt and get an idea. "Ben, I need you to keep firing, while I try to stop it all."

"Sure thing," Ben says while he moves in a circular pattern so he can shoot in all directions. I pull off all my grenades from my belt and attach them in sets. I take two, pull the pin from them, and throw them in the direction of a group of soldiers. The explosion pushed Ben and I to the ground along with other soldiers, but we got back up quickly enough to not get shot. I pulled the pin from my second batch of grenades and threw this set in the opposite direction to what I threw the other. It causes another explosion knocking Ben and me down. But we once again got up in time. My final batch. I swing it around my head, as high as I can. Then I send them into the crowd of soldiers.

Jeremiah Anderson

The explosion becomes the largest of them all, the collision with the ones I threw and the grenades on the soldier's belts throws Ben and I across the field into a building. I get back up to see if there is anyone else coming for us, but everyone appears to be dead or injured. Everyone looks harmless. Ben stands back up, stretching his back and looking around trying to figure out what happened.

Ben stumbles over to me placing his hand on my head. "Dude… Next time a warning please," Ben says trying to stand up straight, without falling to the ground again.

"Next time be ready," I say as I run over to a large building that looks a lot like the one from the last base we were at. I enter the room, wander around a little, and find it to be no different than the last place. I found an office with a book on the desk. Ben pulls out a translator book and gets cracking on decoding the first page.

I wait patiently by looking through the books on the shelf, unable to read them of course. They contain what appear to be children's stories. I look through the pages trying to understand what is happening. I find them quite interesting. I place the book back on the shelf and turn to Ben to find out if he is done, but I find him to be hazy and bumping around into things. He looked out of breath, so I sat him down in a chair.

"So, what did you find?" I ask I want to help him, but I don't know if I can without knowing what he found.

"Kek... Kek Voronin. He wrote this book." He continues to proceed with explaining what he found. This is what he said.

Kek is one of the three Soviet World Condemners. They have disbanded the Russian military and created their own secret group to attack the other countries of the world. They have hit America, England, Australia, and Brazil. They plan to take over these places since they are the most powerful countries in each continent. They will not rest until they have made the world their playground. They also have other things I haven't any idea about. Like how they have this machine that changes your brain waves. Causing you to relive whatever you hide from. You will relive your worst mistakes. Your worst fears. Your worst nightmares.

I understand why Ben is worried. If we fail, then the whole world is at risk. If we destroy their resources, we can win this thing. If they can't eat or have enough ammo to fight. They will be forced to retreat. Thankfully Kek is dead, so I don't have to worry about him coming for us.

Ben stands up, grabs the book, and walks out of the room. I follow him trying to figure out why he is storming off like this. A soldier jumps out of nowhere and aims at Ben. More than ready to kill him. I pull out my gun but I'm too slow, Ben shoots the soldier's leg before I can decide where to shoot.

Ben turns his head and faces me removing his mask. "Let's finish this thing," he says in a commanding voice. He shoves open the door and shoots two more soldiers that were trying to jump at us. I froze in shock at how determined Ben is to finish this thing. Regardless I ran out the door for Ben and found him halfway to the exit of the base. He places bombs and grenades along with other explosives in crates as he walks past. I catch up to Ben and help him lay the explosives down. When we get to the gate, Ben pulls out a grenade and pulls the pin, giving it a little kiss, he throws it into the base. Blowing it to pieces.

I removed my mask and placed my hand on Ben's shoulder to comfort him. "We will finish this, and everything and everyone will be okay," I say softly. We make fists to give each other a bump on the back of the hand and run for the final base.

Shadow Venom

The base is larger than any other base we have ever been to, so we observe the base silently behind a bush. Ben hides the book under a large rock and then focuses on how to get inside. I look closely and notice that the gate is open in the front, and there are no guards present. I take this as a sign to enter through there. I rush over to the gate and peek through it before entering the base. No soldiers are within sight, so Ben and I proceed quickly and quietly. We climb a tall guard tower, and when we get to the top, we find there to be no guards present in it either.

I begin to wonder why we haven't seen any soldiers here yet, then I look out of the window of the guard tower, and I don't find a single human being in the entire base.

Chapter 20

We climbed down from the tower to look for the main headquarters of the base. We wander through the paved streets looking at all the giant buildings that appear to look like futuristic skyscrapers. There are shops of all sorts and delis along with bakeries. This place is like a minimized city, though it's for the most part the size of one. Ben picks up a brick and carefully aims for a window. I briskly grab his hand before he can throw it. If there is anyone left here, they could have some burglar system and alert them that we are here.

Ben turns to me giving me a small smile. "Don't worry, we'll be fine," he says practically reading my mind. I release my grip on him and give a soft sigh. He throws the brick through the window. Smashing the glass and starting a loud alarm system. I look for anyone who might be heading our way, but not a soul in sight. We enter the shop taking as much food as we can to eat, but also stocking up on our supplies like grenades and bullets. I grab a few bottles of butane to fill my cartridges, so I can use my flame emitter. I leave the shop to look around the area for a place to blow up the base. But there isn't much military equipment other than the stuff at the front of the base. This place must have been where they get most of their resources, and the other bases are the actual military bases. But if we can destroy this Soviet World Condemners thing, we will win this thing, and everything will go back to normal. Well as normal as things can be.

I continue to walk up the road as Ben catches up to me. I turn my head to see what he is carrying, and I'm not surprised to find he has half the shop's food supply in his bag. I figure if these guys are giving up and running away, then we might as well take their food, so it doesn't go to waste.

We wandered the streets for a few more minutes before finding the very building we were searching for. The base's central headquarters. We both entered the building as though we owned the place without worry of soldiers popping out, but as a safety precaution, I held my shield in my hand. The building is very different than the other ones.

This one has a nice crystal chandelier hanging from the ceiling and a carpet that looks like fireworks and seashells. There are plush white chairs that look like they were designed for maximum relaxation. I walk up the stairs in search of the office and I find it rather quickly. The room is covered with gold and other ores. I ran to the desk to find a book resting on the top, but there was none. I take another look throughout the room for the book, but I don't find it. As I'm about to leave when my eyes get caught on something on the wall. There's this map of Long Beach, New York. Ben enters the room and begins to translate the words on the map. I got bored of waiting, so I walked up to him, snatched the book from his hands, and translated it. Ben gives a loud sigh and looks around the room himself.

My eyes widened with shock as I read the translation to Ben. "Ben... it says that the Russians plan to send troops to America for the start, then once they think the time is right, they will desert the bases on Russia and move to America and destroy their largest city and take it hostage and gain control. To crush it," I say as Ben nearly faints on the ground. He looks as though he is about to hyperventilate, but he relaxes himself before we get that far.

Could this be a good thing? Now we know where all the members of this group are, or at least where they are heading. Which means we can stop them in time. We can end this. End the madness. Before it ends me.

Shadow Venom

He takes a deep breath trying to focus his thoughts. "Then we better get back if we are their only hope," Ben says. I give him a nod showing I understand. We sit here feeling defeated, and almost feeling as though we've lost this thing from the beginning. But I won't stand for it. I reach my hand down offering Ben a hand up, he gracefully accepts it standing up. We ran back downstairs as we both threw grenades behind us. Blowing up the building. The sight of the base reminds me of the mission. I realize the mission isn't complete until I make it home and destroy the Russian forces. I climb to the top of a nearby building, feeling the breeze in my hair and the cold breeze biting me throughout my body. I see a runway not far from where I am, so I yell down to alert Ben of it. I climbed back down with haste and ran for the runway. Ben follows close behind, struggling to keep up. When we reach the runway, we find that a barbed wire gate separates us from accessing the place.

I start to get a look in my eye, so Ben walks over to me and places his hand on my shoulder. "Why don't we climb the fence, they aren't that hard to climb," he suggested. Pushing Ben aside, I ran away from the fence and unclipped a grenade. And pulled the pin out. When I'm about to throw it, Ben grabs my hand preventing me from throwing it. "You don't need to cause so much destruction."

Ignoring what he said. I threw the grenade into the fence, blowing a hole in it, so I could walk through. Ben sighs in grief but continues to follow me through the fence anyway.

I look for an aircraft to use to fly back to New York with, but I see none sitting on the runway, although I do notice a hangar nearby. Ben runs ahead of me for it, and we both race each other across the runway for the hangar. He has the lead momentarily, but I change that quickly by passing him. Without even trying. Ben swiftly gains speed and catches up with me. I run faster until I've hit my limit, as does Ben. Pushing myself harder until I'm barely a foot ahead of Ben. It was exhausting. But I make it to the hangar before him. He falls into the snow with a big laugh. I laugh as well with joy. A joy that wasn't gone. Just forgotten. The childish happiness reminds me of what it was like before the invasion. Ben and I could have spent all that day having fun without a worry in sight. My father and his could have come home and shooed us out of the room as they talked. But instead, my father died, and his father survived. I hate to think something like this.

But why his?

Shadow Venom

My father was a wonderful man who had nothing but the intention to do right in mind, Ben's father murdered people for money. My face frowns at the thought of this, a small tear runs down my face in the sorrow of my father.

Ben notices my sadness and gets up patting me on the back. "Hey man, I wish fate would have let us stay kids, instead we now must be the world's most dangerous soldiers. When we get back if everything works out. I want to spend every last second of my life being a normal kid with you," says Ben, as his smile comforts my sadness. We both continue into the hangar to look for some sort of aircraft to use to escape this frozen hell. Ben quickly finds a plane. I can tell because he's jumping up and down like some little kid.

I run over to the plane to check it out, as I'm looking under the plane, I find keys sitting on the floor next to it. Ben's currently in the cockpit, so I am trying to figure out how he got in. I looked around the side and found this sliding door. I enter the aircraft and find white leather seats with drinks and food all around. The silver lining on all the utensils. The diamond rings and jewelry that just lie on the counters. All this shows how rich these guys must have been. This jet is nicer than my house. Or what was left of it? I toss Ben the keys to start it up as I look around the outside of the plane to make sure we won't go into flames while we're in flight. But everything looks like it is okay for the flight. I'm no pilot, but I'm hoping that we can get this thing going.

I entered the plane again to find Ben playing in the cockpit. "Hey Mr. Pilot, your plane is a little low on fuel, better fill up the tank."

Ben stands up and turns around giving me a salute. "Aye aye captain," says Ben as he rushes out to fill up the tank. I look around the plane for anything that might be useful like another secret book. The plane has an interesting smell to it that I haven't smelled anywhere else I can't seem to figure out what it is. I found a small compartment with guns and other weapons, probably used in case they were ever attacked. Unfortunately, they won't only be attacked by me. But slaughtered.

I sit down on the bed and open the nightstand. I find books inside with American children's stories. Next to them was a translator of Russian to English. I also found another red book. It has a symbol that I don't recognize on it. It seems to look like a scorpion. I open the book to see the name *Sergey Petrov* printed on the front page. Translating the book, I can read that he has many experiments that he's working on. Some of them sound quite dreadful, like the fact that he created a chemical that causes you to forget things. Such as people, places, and even periods of time. He also has experimented with chemicals that can change your personality.

Closer to the end of the book he talks about how he had done experiments on animals to cause them to become more aggressive towards their own species to the point of cannibalism. They don't appear to consider their actions as against their instinct; they simply attack whatever is around them.

Terrifying.

~

After sleeping on the couch in the plane for a couple of hours, I'm awakened when Ben reports to me that he's completed refueling the plane.

"Mission completed sir," Ben says giving me another salute. I return his salute and go on to check the front of the plane to see if it says that we are completely refueled. I am happy to find out it is. Ben and I quickly ran to the doors of the hangar to close them. Once they were completely closed, Ben and I prepared the plane for takeoff, he latched the door shut as I read a manual for flying the plane. I don't get far in it, but I figure I should be fine since I shouldn't have to worry about requesting American towers for landing since they probably aren't going to do anything anyway.

Ben puts on his seat belt and gives me a thumbs up and a nod expressing he's ready for takeoff. I put my seat belt on and started up the engines. I slowly turned the yoke causing the plane to move forward out of the hangar and onto the runway. I center it as well as I can, before stopping the plane.

"You ready?" I asked Ben.

"Ready as I'll ever be," says Ben. We both turn white with fear as I increase the speed of the airplane. I gradually pulled back on the yoke lifting us off the ground more and more by the second. Ben holds onto his seat for dear life, as I am having fun but also terrified at the same time. The end of the runway approaches I feel as though we're not going to make it, so I pull back harder on the yoke. We make it into the air, but the mountain surrounds us. I turn the yoke to dodge the mountain. The wing gets close to the mountain, but I managed to clear the ridged and rocky terrain in time. Using the navigator, we manage to fly steady in the air for a little while, but it takes even longer for me to trust the plane enough to use the autopilot. I stand up to stretch my legs and walk around a little bit. Ben pulls out all the food he can and devours it like a pig.

Shadow Venom

The pudding falls down his face dripping into his mashed potatoes. The turkey leg pieces fly everywhere as he bites into it, and he hasn't even considered reaching for a napkin.

"Dude, you're disgusting," I say feeling nauseated.

"What I haven't eaten well in a long time," says Ben as he throws more food in his mouth. I understand what he means, neither have I, but feeling disgusted I leave that area of the plane to the bedroom to sleep in. I feel uncomfortable with leaving the cockpit unattended, but at this point, I don't care. I don't want to walk back out and have to look at Ben eating again. So, I forget about it and go to sleep.

~

My rest was peaceful and undisturbed. I walk out of the bedroom bracing myself to watch Ben eat again, but he isn't present in the main cabin. I walk into the cockpit and find him sitting in the copilot seat watching the flashing buttons making sure we aren't going to crash.

"So, you done eating like a pig?" I ask hoping for a response that doesn't involve me feeling nauseous.

"Nope," he says throwing another grape into his mouth.

I almost frown at his response, but I guess it's fair.

We sit silently in the cockpit for a few minutes looking ahead of us out the window, staring at the clouds and the waves below. I feel like we should talk, but I don't know what there is to discuss. After a few minutes, I gathered enough courage to start a conversation, but Ben started one before I could.

"So, how many nightmares have you had?" Ben asks. "About killing people. I mean. Since the whole invasion of the Russian terrorists."

I find that to be a strange question, but I decided to answer anyway. "Just the one, you?"

"I've had quite a few," Ben says to my surprise.

My eyes widen in shock. "Of killing people? You're practically harmless to all these guys."

"But before." It takes a few moments for me to figure out what he means, and then I remember that he slaughtered half the kids on our block. "I had a dream that I fell into the carpet in some kids' room. When I hit the bottom, all the kids I killed were in there. Pulling me to the bottom. I tried to get out, but they pulled me down into the horde of them, their necks were ripped out just as I killed them. I had that one for many nights and a few others, and then I discovered that you were the Shadow Venom. I realized that I nearly killed my best friend. I decided that it doesn't matter the reason, killing isn't right. It's something that I feel shouldn't be justified," says Ben curdling in fear.

"I'm sorry, but you stopped doing that. Now you can kill for good, instead of evil," I say enthusiastically.

"What no!" Ben says jumping up. "I don't want to kill at all. I can't justify killing, no one can." Ben says lifting his voice.

"What why?" I asked in confusion. He had been willing to kill innocent children but not dangerous soldiers.

"I don't want to kill people, okay?"

"You've changed so much, the Ben I knew wouldn't have any problem fighting for justice," I say rising in anger, slamming my hands down on a table.

Jeremiah Anderson

"Well guess what Hunter, this has changed me. It has changed you. I have changed myself through this. At least I've changed into someone who wants to find a way to win without causing harm to people. I don't care about a victory in this. I just want people to stop dying. You want to murder everyone because you're in pain and don't know how to handle it. So, you've changed into the very things that changed you, the thing you despise," says Ben as he storms off back into the cabin. His anger and rage are still fresh in my mind. The way his veins popped. The redness of his eyes. His ability to get so mad that he sweats.

I sat there in disbelief of what he had said. Because I know who I am now. I have become stronger and not afraid to get things done. I have the will to complete my mission and that mission I will complete. I have become a ruthless monster. But if that's what the Russian terrorists will fear, then that's what I'll be. I have become someone who can take away everything from them like how they took everything away from me.

My anger will not be satisfied until I have taken everything away from them as they did me. I will have their blood.

Every. Last. Drop.

Shadow Venom

Part 4

"Revelation."

Shadow Venom

Chapter 21

I walk into the cabin and sit down beside Ben. "Can I ask you something without either of us getting mad?" I request.

Ben looks at me with mad teary eyes. "Sure," says Ben, nodding his head. I know that he isn't doing well after killing innocent people, so I feel as though I need to help him out a bit, come to a mutual agreement even.

I take a deep breath. "So, I think that I have become someone stronger, faster, and even better than before. I think that you have become weak and unwilling to do what is necessary for us to triumph. I want to know your perspective." I've decided to try and get things a little better between us because if we aren't getting along here it will be that much more dangerous when fighting the Russian soldiers.

Shadow Venom

Ben looks at me taking a deep breath then exhaling loudly. "Well, you might see yourself as some hero, as someone doing the right thing. Look at yourself, you're a monster. You've become what you despise, you've become the evil that changed you," he says almost with anger, which is what I was hoping to avoid. "You can be like me instead. Not a weak person, but someone who wants to change things for the better. You don't have to cause so much suffering and pain. You're mad and you want to hurt them, you don't need to be the darkness within that changed you. You're a monster, not a hero." I open my mouth trying to say something, but Ben senses that and speaks before I can even make a sound. "And if you're trying to patch things up, so we don't disagree on the field to make it safer," Ben gets up and places his hand on my shoulders. "You're still my best friend and always will be. I won't let anything happen to either of us."

It's nice to know that he can read my mind and everything, but it doesn't necessarily help us any. He's been saying the same thing repeatedly. I try to see his point of view, but I don't understand why he wouldn't want to make them pay for what they've done to us. They stole our lives. I only want to give them a taste of what that's like.

Jeremiah Anderson

Ben leaves the room without further comment, and heads to the bedroom to get some rest, and give me space. I decided to go get some more rest in the main pilot's seat up front in the cockpit.

~

After a few hours, I am awakened by Ben. New York is in view. My eyes widen with excitement. I figured that it would be difficult to land the plane on the beach, so Ben and I decided to use a couple of parachutes to get back to the ground. I am shocked Ben agreed to let the plane go wherever it goes, destroying the forest, but I guess he is starting to see reason. Ben hands me a parachute and helps to attach everything to me before starting on himself. I offered to help him, but he refused. We ready ourselves next to the door of the plane getting ready to jump. Ben opens the latch to the door and pulls it open. I look down and suddenly have this sense of fear come over me, pulling me away from the door, it's strange since I'm not afraid of heights. I ignore it and prepare to jump.

Ben pushes me aside and stands ready to jump first. I figure it doesn't matter who goes first. As I wait for Ben to jump, he grabs my hand and jumps. Forcing me out the door as well.

Shadow Venom

Ben is quick to open his parachute and start slowly descending. As quickly as I can I do the same, so we reach the bottom around the same time.

It feels as though I get tugged by a magnet away from Ben. I look up to see what's going on and I see Ben's parachute fly right into the plane's turbine. Pulling Ben away from me and right into the turbine. His blood splatters all over me. It's in my mouth and eyes. I can taste his skin and smell his hair. Ben always had my back. Now I have his. All over mine.

I just lost my best friend right in front of my eyes.

I dive down hoping to avoid the same death Ben did. My chest suddenly has humongous pain come over it, my hand reaches for my chest hoping to stop the pain, but of course, nothing changes. I truly comprehend and realize now that Ben is dead, my mind starts to feel this shift, like some sort of realization coming over it. I can't figure out what it's about, but it's there.

I started to wonder if I caused this. If it were my choices that caused Ben's death. Could I have prevented this if I had made the right choice?

The plane follows me down. How? That's impossible. I'm no pilot, but it shouldn't be following me like this. I took my dagger, and I cut the ropes holding me in place. and dive down hoping to hit the water. But I that realize even if I hit the water the impact with kill me. The molecules in the water won't have time to separate. It would be like hitting concrete. I pull the string releasing the safety parachute from my pack. Right when I think I'm safe the plane gets too close, and the turbine tears my parachute apart, destroying it.

The turbine slowly sucks me in. I try to cut myself loose, but I can't in time, the turbine is almost a foot away. I try to duck hoping it would help, but the plane picks up speed, getting closer and closer until… I woke up.

I'm covered in sweat. I'm panting hard, harder than I ever have before. Ben sits next to me peeling a banana, paying attention to me.

"What happened?" I asked, looking around the cockpit trying to figure out if this was real or not.

Ben looks at me, showing that he expected this. "You had a nightmare. Probably about someone close to you dying, right?" Ben asks, as my jaw drops, and my eyes widen. He knows something that I don't. I want to know how he knows this.

"When I was killing people I got nightmares, terrible nightmares. It started as me being in danger of who I killed, then it moved on to those that were close to me being killed," says Ben slouching in his seat. I turn my head away since I don't want to start feeling bad for him, if I spend my brain power feeling bad for him, then I might find myself being as harmless to the enemy as he is, and I won't accomplish my mission.

"Or maybe my mind is preparing me to be ready for anything that comes my way," I exclaimed. I can tell Ben didn't buy one bit of it. He practically ignored it.

Ben exhales. "Believe what you want, but just think about this," says Ben, probably going to tell me killing is wrong or repeat some other lame thing he has previously said. "Imagine if Chloe knew what you were doing. Imagine if your former self knew what you were doing. Imagine if your family knew what you were doing. You don't need to kill to set things right, you can become the person to prevent this from happening because you're only continuing the evil. Your job as the hero is supposed to stop it. End it," Ben states as he walks out of the cockpit and back into the cabin. What he said almost makes sense. I think about it for a moment, before shaking it off.

New York is in sight. Only for real this time. I ran to get Ben in the cabin to find him already suited up in a parachute. With a bag full of food and his weapons. I almost walk over to get a parachute for myself before remembering my nightmare.

My whole body freezes with shock. "Can we maybe try to land the plane in the water instead of jumping out the door?" I asked Ben, with a clear fear of jumping from the plane.

"I understand," Ben says taking off the parachute. "It was me, wasn't it?" Once again, he reads my mind. Both of us ran up to the cockpit, buckling in and getting ready to land this thing. I steered down close to the water, but not touching it. Slowly turning off the ignition. I slowed the plane down enough that we might be able to make a safe landing on the water.

Ben and I slip on our masks, so when we get off if someone catches us, they don't see our real faces. The plane lands in the water stopping any further movement from it. Ben and I quickly grabbed the bags he laid out and opened the door. The cabin quickly floods. We act fast, swimming out of the plane and into the open water. We headed for Long Beach.

Waves shove us around the place, and sometimes into each other. I would consider leaving the bags, but if they didn't have food and other things we need like our weapons, I would simply let them go.

Shadow Venom

Crawling onto the beach feels as though it is the most difficult thing yet. I'm drenched and tired, though I got hours of sleep on the plane. Ben gives me a hand up, and we both continue into the forest to get back to Mark and alert him of the news that we discovered.

Chapter 22

It was a nice cool morning, so we spent a few hours hiking through the forest next to the river. I'm glad to be back home. The cold in Russia was killer. Ben often requests to remove his mask, but I keep him from doing so since I don't want either of our identities to be discovered. Especially since everyone else thinks he's dead. He's basically a ghost.

We walk through the forest until we reach the small raft that Ben and I made a little while ago. I drag it into the water while Ben walks through the forest looking for some berries. I refuse to believe that this is real and when Ben finds the berries I will know.

The raft feels like it might fall apart soon, but I put it in the water anyway. I look for something to use as paddles. Without having enough time to make a good set of paddles some long sticks should work. I attached a few more sticks to the raft to make it stronger, as well as tied many other things like pinecones, twigs, and pine needles to the raft to increase the buoyancy.

Ben returns running through the forest. "Hunter, Hunter look," Ben says with his hands covered in a bright red color, I glance over it for a second getting back to work. It takes a few moments before realizing that my hands are covered in a bright red liquid. As I look back Ben faints to the ground. I hear gunshots off in the distance. Ben has been shot. By the Russians? It doesn't matter right now. I need to get him to safety. I threw him behind my neck and over my shoulders ignoring the raft. He weighs me down, but I use all my strength to carry him through the forest, running as fast as possible. I listen to the firing as it gets stronger and stronger. The amount of gunfire gradually increases until it sounds as though an entire army is chasing us. I jump over logs and small streams that block my way.

I have no sense of direction to where I'm heading. I try to run as far away from the shooters as possible. The branches smack me in the face, feeling like whips, but I ignore the pain, because if I get captured. I will be in infinite pain. Up ahead, I see an area where the tree's part, and I can get through easily. I expect to find some open ground that I can use to shoot and fight the

Russians, but instead, a massive drop down to a river appears below. They quickly get closer. I need to make a decision fast. The firing ends. I still can't see soldiers anywhere, but I assume they are trying to sneak up on us. So, I decided to jump. I take a few steps back so I can jump as far as possible.

I ran with all my might and launched myself from the edge, and onto the hill I hadn't seen before. Ben and I rolled down the hill hitting many bushes and nearly hitting the trees growing on the hill. Ben must have been in extreme pain since he was shot, and I don't even know where. We splash into the water hitting the river floor. I'm too tired to move, so I keep hold of Ben and hold him above the water and let the water take me wherever. I don't care as long as it's away from the soldiers.

We rode the river current until we both landed on the riverbank. Ben and I lay there unable to move. Ben is barely conscious. I hear soldiers approaching from the forest, I don't see them. But my ears can pick up what my eyes can't.

I slowly stood back up pushing Ben down into the water to conceal him a little more. "Don't worry Ben. I won't let them hurt you," I exclaimed aloud to Ben, not caring about whether someone heard or not. Tears run down my face, knowing that at least one of us will lose their life. I'm the only one who has a chance, but I can't leave my best friend here. I struggled to pull my katana out and hold my shield in my hand. The weight draws me back to the floor, the floor I must resist if I'm to protect Ben, as well as myself. I stand ready to attack, but everything is dizzy, and I feel off balance. I try to focus but nothing is working.

The soldiers are approaching. They are wearing something completely different than usual, and one of them appears to be shouting at me. I can't make out what he's saying, but I assume it's bad. I raise my katana in the air and swing at one of the soldiers, but he stops it with his hand. Without any effort.

He bends down, I suspect to kill me. "Son, it's me," he says kindly and sincerely.

I try to focus my mind on what's happening.

"It's me, Mark." Mark? It's Mark. He's come to help me, but why did he shoot Ben? I attempt to ask these questions, but before I can speak.

I blacked out.

~

Jeremiah Anderson

My eyelids slowly open, revealing me to be back at the shelter. I sat up looking around trying to find some clue as to what happened. I look down and find my clothes to have been changed, into a grey pair of pants and a green shirt. I jumped out of bed and found a closet with a note on it, it was from Mark. I read it, and this is what he said.

Hey Kid,

I hid your suit in the closet, but I told everyone that I found you playing in the river, and you got lost. So, no one would figure out who you are.

I must say that I do appreciate the fact that he helps me out with this secret identity thing. I truly appreciate it, but I want to know why he was shooting at Ben, that reminds me. Ben was shot. I need to make sure he's okay. I might be able to help him. As long as Mark hasn't already killed him.

I ran down the halls looking for Ben. I ran to the main room with all the other refugees. But I assumed Ben wouldn't be in there, so I ignored it and turned to walk away, but Chloe stood right behind me holding a plate of food.

She drops the plate with her eyes wide open and jaw dropped. She suddenly jumps at me hugging me. "I thought you were taken, injured, or worse," she says crying into my shoulder. I returned the hug and gave her a few small pats on the back.

"You can't lose me that easily," I say smugly. She glares at me looking as though she wants to slap me but refusing the urge and stares into my eyes. I pulled her in closer giving her another big hug. At some point, we let go and go our separate ways without saying another word. We haven't communicated that much since the attack. I'm surprised she hasn't left me for some other guy. After focusing my mind on the task at hand, I continued to look for Ben.

I do another lap down the hall and find Mark talking on the phone in his office. "Okay… Yes, let's do that time, yes it will work." Mark looks towards me almost with shock. "Let's do it then, I've got to go now bye." Mark hangs up the phone and then spins around in his chair a few times. After a few spins, he focuses on me. "So, what did you get?" Mark says almost as though he knows something.

I ignore it and decide to answer the question anyway. "So, I learned that they have all immigrated to numerous different countries, and they plan to wipe out New York soon, so I say we try to figure out when," I say.

"I'll get a man on it," Mark says practically as though he practiced saying that.

"Okay… What's going on? Why are you acting like this?" I say interrogatively.

He slouches in his chair looking almost worried. "Chad already gave me the information, but when he finished, he told me that you might have wanted to give the information. So, I should act as though I never knew," Mark says with slight fright. I almost get upset, but it strikes me that Ben is alive, so I quickly jolt out of the room to look for Ben.

I still want to know what the call was about because I feel something else is up. I run down the hall until I find the room with Ben in it.

Ben has his suit removed as well. I hope no one saw him. But that isn't my biggest concern. I ran up to Ben and gave him a strong hug, knowing that I could lose him for real.

"Hey, you good? What's with all the hugging?" Bens asks confusingly. I guess he might not remember that he nearly died.

"What? I can't give my friend who nearly died a hug?" I ask.

Shadow Venom

"Nearly died?" Ben questions, his eyes widen in shock and his face turns to shame. "Yeah, I a... Nearly died," he said turning his head away and walking away in the opposite direction, attempting to avoid me. But with only so many places he can go and not get caught being a walking dead man, he can't get away.

"Okay spill it, buddy," I commanded him, knowing that he was hiding something.

"So, remember when I passed out after I got your attention?" Ben asks, reminding me of when the soldiers chased us through the forest.

"Yes," I reply.

"The blood on my hands... wasn't mine. There was one of Mark's men who had been shot, and I tried to help him then Russians tried to shoot the rest of us, so I ran back to warn you. But before I could say anything..."

"Before you could say anything?" I ask, trying to keep him on track.

"I fainted at the sight of the blood," Ben says so fast I was barely able to understand. But I understood enough to not know whether to laugh or slap him.

Jeremiah Anderson

"You're in the middle of a war and you faint at the sight of blood? You literally ripped people's throats out." I look at him almost laughing, still feeling a little angry. Ben silently stands there even wondering how he fainted himself.

I throw my hands onto my face wondering what to make of this. "What am I going to do with you?" I ask.

I gave him a light slap across the face because of how pathetic it was. "You're an idiot," I say laughingly. Ben bursts up laughing with joy, I can't help but join him in one of the few moments of happiness that we have left. I hear the door close behind me. I jump around quickly to see who it is, and I find Mark panting. "What's wrong?" I asked worried.

"One of our Strike Back Stingers soldiers attacked the others and killed five of my men," Mark pauses in disappointment, unsure how to continue. "He was a soldier undercover, and I need something of you. And that's for you, to teach the rest of my men how to fight the way you do. They share all your weapons, other than what you have on your left forearm. Train them please." Mark rushes out of the room as though he has somewhere important to be, which he might. I ignore it whilst having the sudden new fear of there being any other undercover Russians, waiting to attack.

Shadow Venom

I headed back to my room to change back into my suit, then headed outside to look for the Strike Back Stingers training area. I look around and see a rack of guns along with shields, swords, and all sorts of other things that are lying around here. The ground is covered in hay, and there's a wooden fence barely standing going around the area. I walk over to the table with ammo, reload my weapons, and store a few ammo cartridges on my belt. A few soldiers look at me almost as though they find it rude that I'm taking their ammo, it may be, but I'm supposed to train them, so this can be payment.

I walk to the center of the training area and look around to see what kind of men I must deal with. "Line up!" I command the soldiers. They all lined up facing me, standing at attention. I walk down the line of them and look around to choose someone. When I've found the man, I stop in front of him and direct him to where I want him to go. He rushes there without question. I set up a few targets for him to shoot. He pulls out the gun on his back, it's rather large and he isn't using a shield like some of the others. I suppose everyone has preferences.

The man aims for the target taking a little while to ready his aim. He pulls the trigger sending the bullet flying, it misses the target by a few feet. I look at him again, ready to send him back, but he quickly prepares another shot. Before I can stop him, he makes an instant bullseye. He was trying to lower my expectations. I stand almost impressed.

I consider taking my mask off, but if one of them is someone who wants to kill me or if they don't wind up dying in battle then I don't want others to know who I am.

"Line up along the fence all of you, I want you all to shoot the targets until you've hit a bullseye," I command. They all run to the fence and shoot the targets, most of them miss but a couple shoot a bullseye on their first shot. When they finish shooting, I round everyone up in a circle. With six guys it's kind of hard to do but I suppose that I will make do with what I have.

"I want all of you to pick a partner and prepare to stand in the center, to fight each other… to the death!"

Chapter 23

I looked around to find every one of them shocked by what I had said. I give a small chuckle, causing them to stare in confusion. They look at me as though they are ready to attack me, seeing as I seem to find this funny. "I'm joking," I affirm them. "But you are all to fight each other. I want to see skills. Choose your choice of weapons. Personalize yourselves," I said.

They all line up in pairs, preparing to fight. The first pair both choose katanas to use, their battle doesn't end without some bloodshed. It ends once one of the fighters holds the sword to the other's neck. I give them a nod in contentment, allowing them to move on and to let the next group through.

The second pair runs up into the center and begins after a firm handshake. Their chosen weapons were daggers. I am intrigued to see their fight. They fight much longer than the last group, but both are far more talented. I ended up sitting down to watch them since they were taking so long. They finally end when one of them takes the dagger from the other and stabs the knife through his uniform into the ground. I give them both a short applause and signal for the next duo.

One of the soldiers chooses numerous weapons whilst the other only uses a shield. I almost let them move on without giving them a chance to fight, but I let them proceed anyway. Surprisingly their fight ends quickly. The man with the shield was so fast that he blocked every attack from the other man and took the other guy down practically without trying.

"That was too easy give me a real challenge. Like taking on everyone at once," the man said, certain he will win. I gave him a gentle nod informing him I would allow it. When they start, he plows through everyone, like a tractor through a field of corn. I consider stopping him, but I'm curious about his strength. He doesn't stop to let others have a chance to catch a breath, instead, he knocks everyone to the ground, leaving them practically paralyzed, and unable to fight.

"Hey, how about you fight me? Or are you too scared," I ask smugly.

"Oh, I'll destroy you," the man says, expecting some weak kid.

Shadow Venom

"Let's see about that," I say. I tighten my suit, preparing myself to fight. I noticed he only had a shield, and it would be too easy to win if I had all my gear, so I removed everything except my electrified venom shocker, and my shield. We both stand only a few feet apart ready to fight. One of the soldiers blows a horn unexpectedly, and the man charges in and tries to decapitate me with his shield. I block before he manages to. He turns back around for another go, but before he can lay a hit on me, I sweep his feet causing him to fall over.

Suddenly, everything changes, I'm back in the relaxation gardens, it seems so peaceful. But moments later the ground burns up, killing all the life surrounding it, and causing cracks in the building. A figure immersed in the smoke. It's Ben. But not as Ben. It's him as the Dark Condemner. He holds a shield in his hands, ready to kill me. He leaps up at me. I hold my shield up, but that's not enough to stop his attack, he shoves me into the ground. Wait. I can taste the dirt, maybe this is real. I rise back up, but suddenly he disappears, then reappears and hits me on the back of the head. I fell to the ground again, scared and confused. I know I must be seeing things again, but what if I'm not? What if this is real? I decided to fight. Every attack of his feels stronger, and more powerful than before. "Ben it's me, it's me Ben!" I call out, hoping that he will give some response, and stop trying to kill me. It doesn't work, he only gets stronger, he senses my fear, and he feeds on it. I can't give in.

I must win. Or it could mean imminent death. I don't know anymore.

He sends many swings at my face trying to hit me, I step back more and more until I can't take it anymore. "Enough!" I yell at the top of my lungs. I turn on my electrified venom shocker to a higher setting than usual. He sends his shield flying down at my head, but I use all my strength to catch it.

"Enough," I say in a cold and raspy voice. I send my strongest punch into him, blasting him away from me. Everything comes back to me. I'm back in the training field. I watch as the soldier flies into a pile of hay and bricks. I stand almost appalled by the fact I was tricked by my own mind again. I can't let this happen again. I gear up and move back inside the shelter to get out of the area, I don't bother to let everyone know that training is done. I walk inside and find everyone in a rush. I can't tell why. But I see this man lying down on a bed in need of immediate medical attention, which he's getting.

Shadow Venom

Mark talks to him as the nurses and doctors try to heal the man's wounds. I wonder who it is and why this has happened to him. I take a few more steps closer hoping to get a better look, but someone shoves me away and places a curtain around the man.

After waiting a couple of hours for Mark to finish talking to the man, Mark walks out from the curtain. "Hey son, so how's the training?" Mark asks exhaustedly.

"Not the worst," I reply. May not be the best time to tell him I nearly killed someone. "What's going on with that man?" I ask curiously.

Mark looks at me with sorrow in his eyes. "That man was undercover hiding in a Russian base. After Chad told me about the situation of the attack from Russia coming soon, I sent that soldier on a mission to find out when. Well after he received the message, they somehow discovered he was undercover and attacked him, he made it back here without being followed, and got the information we needed." He pauses, clearly feeling guilty for the man's death. "They're attacking tomorrow night, so you rest up because that's when we'll finish this thing," Mark says. Trying to understand that there's nothing he can do to help the man anymore. "Got that son?"

"Yes. I do. I'll see to it that Chad rests too," I say, leaving to go get some rest.

I find Ben sitting on his bed. Bouncing a ball off the floor into the wall and back into his hands. He doesn't even look to see who enters the room, instead, he continues to bounce his ball off the ground. I sit next to him on the bed and watch as he bounces the ball. Feeling unsafe to sleep anywhere without someone watching. I decided to sleep on Ben's bed, as he played with the ball.

I'm shaken awake by Mark, he places his finger on his mouth, telling me I need to stay silent. "We figured out the exact location that they will attack from. If we can reach the bridge before them, we might be able to blow it up. And hopefully trap them," Mark whispers. "But I can't go... I a... have some other matters to attend to," he says mysteriously. I assume he wants it silent, so Ben can't hear, I look over my shoulder and see him lying against the wall sleeping.

"So, when do we need to leave?" I ask.

"Very soon," Mark rushes. "We need to pack up immediately and prepare to fight. I gave directions to my number two, Jason Mycroft. On the where and when," Mark explained. I don't hesitate to follow directions. Mark runs out of the room, but not before looking both ways to make sure the coast is clear. Ben wakes up from the slam of the door, and by the stare in my eyes, he knows to get ready.

When Bens finishes putting his suit on, we both head out to grab some food before we leave. I became curious about how the public with act if they were to see Ben, or "The Dark Condemner."

So, to test what happens, I walk Ben fully suited into the line to get food, it would look too strange if I weren't also suited up. So, I made a quick stop in my room to get dressed. When I finished, we got in line. We both looked like we were going to a costume party. People look relieved that he is on our side, but at the same time, they are keeping a twenty-foot distance.

After we finish eating, we both go our separate ways to say goodbye, since there is a chance that both of us don't make it back alive. Ben gets his mother's attention and signals to meet somewhere private. Probably, so he can take his mask off. I look for my mother, I don't expect to die, so I don't need somewhere private, plus to make things look less suspicious. I'll say goodbye to a bunch of random people.

Jeremiah Anderson

After barely escaping a conversation with a man I was saying goodbye to, I find my mother and stand next to her. Attempting not to look at her. "So, I guess this is goodbye," I say, she doesn't make it look like she is talking to me either, so I understand she gets what I'm trying to do.

"I suppose so, but can you remember one thing for me?" She asks.

"Sure, what's that?" I asked. She turns around, ignoring my discreet goodbye, and hugs me.

She wraps me tight in her arms. "Try to forget who you've become and try to remember who you are," She gives me one last tight squeeze before walking away. I wonder why she could be saying that it caused me to ponder it, but I instantly forget when I remember that I need to focus on the mission. I walked back over to the place Ben, and I ate, patiently waiting for him to return. He takes a little longer than expected, probably since he figures he may not survive this fight, especially if he won't kill anyone.

I feel a poke on my arm, so I turn to see what it is, and I find Ben hiding behind a trash can. I don't bother to ask why. I tilt my head confused with why he is doing that. But before I could ask, he signaled for the exit.

Shadow Venom

We both walked towards the door without any issues. I expected at least one person to stop us, but no one seemed to be interested enough to care. We pick up speed, and as I am about to climb out Chloe stops us. She doesn't make eye contact but moves in closer to give us both a hug. She lifts both of our masks enough to give us both a small kiss on the cheek. We all place our foreheads up against each other's. We all know this is the last time that we will be together. It's clear Chloe knows our identities, but the question is how.

Chloe walked away before I got the chance to ask, so Ben and I continued with what we were doing and climbed out. The second we land our feet outside the building; we find who I assume is Jason waiting right outside the entrance. He doesn't say anything, merely directs us to the jeeps. We spend a few minutes loading the jeeps so that Mark's men have what they need. After we finished, we rode off to finish this war.

~

The ride is silent for the most part, every now and again the jeep will sputter. I think everybody is trying to stay quiet, so they can focus on getting ready to fight. They know that most of them will end up dead. I would offer to fight this fight alone, but we all know that this is our battle. Not one single man's alone. So, I understand why these men are willing to give their lives.

The sky begins to darken. Revealing the one thing that I will use to finish this war. The darkness. My most powerful weapon. A weapon that can be used for or against me, it all depends on how I wield it.

Ben turns to me giving a loud exhale, indicating he's about to talk. "What are you thinking about?" he asks. "How to win this thing peacefully, I assume not."

I turn to him with slight outrage. "I will not let a single Russian live, I want them to suffer as I did!" I call out to Ben. I can't believe that we are doing this now, before the big fight.

Ben hesitates to lash back out at me but remains calm. "Well just don't become them, because you believe justice is your motive."

"It is!" I announce.

"No." Ben pauses. "It's hatred and anger," Ben states. "Hate and anger will control you, and it will destroy not only you but everyone else around you," Ben pauses holding himself back. "Even those that you care about, including the ones you want to save."

Shadow Venom

"The enemy will suffer, everyone else will be fine," I state. "I have become a better man than I was before, you have become weak and cowardly," I lash out.

"If that's what you want to call it. I simply refuse to kill, if I can escape it then I choose that route. Because I know what it's done to me. It nearly killed me," Ben says, barely above a whisper. I can't believe he would say something like that. I leaned back in shock, he had said it many times before, but this time it hit differently. But what was that feeling I felt when he died in my nightmare? I may never know again. But I do know that because of all of this, I have gained a strength I didn't even know existed in me, a strength that can corrupt every other.

Jeremiah Anderson
Chapter 24

The jeep bounces up and down as it rides over logs and small bumps in the forest. I try to gather my thoughts on the mission ahead, so I can finish this thing as fast as possible. I don't want any casualties. Because I may be able to get most of my life back on track. Ben, on the other hand, will not be given a happy ending after what he did. I still can't believe he's talked to me about mercy when he slaughtered almost every kid on our block, and nearly killed me.

The animals in the forest jump into the bushes and hide away fearing all of mankind and their powerful deadly weapons. Despite the little pain something as little as a wasp could give us we still avoid them at all costs and make sure to not irritate one, but another human on the other hand; we will willingly irritate and go out of our way to harm one even though humans are far more intelligent can cause so much more pain than that wasp.

Shadow Venom

My mind continues to drift until we reach our destination, the bridge. Everyone leaps out of their jeeps and rushes to the other side knowing exactly what to do, working together as a team, a team that might be able to finish this thing. They set a line of explosives along the outside of the bridge hiding them from the naked eye. And another team climbs below the bridge and sets another row of explosives underneath. I entirely understand the plan, so I stand still and watch as everyone else runs around me setting things up and preparing for the final fight.

I walk over to the edge of the bridge to look at the water below, but as I walk over. I tripped on some construction equipment. An idea pops in my head, I figure that I might be able to use some of this in a fight. I might be able to throw the saw blades, so I don't have to waste all my bullets. These soldiers have almost no chance against me, so I may never need them. Ben helps to carry some boxes and other weapons to get things ready for the battle, but if things go south then I need to be ready myself to save everyone. I realize I have a big ego to think that I can win this thing on my own, but so far nothing has shown me that I couldn't. Other than when the Russians captured me and tortured me. For many, many days.

Jeremiah Anderson

Everyone sets up their stations from where they will be firing from. So, when the Russians come. We can kill them straight away. I'm hoping no one accidentally shoots me, that would be a pretty lame death. Killed by my team.

Ben climbs up on top of a jeep and clears his throat. "I know all of you are scared, I know you all want this to be over. But it's not," Ben exclaims. "We have survived this far, who's to say we can't survive a little longer? Who's to say we can't thrive?" Ben asks, causing the crowd to murmur among themselves.

The crowd turns to dead silence and looks at Ben again. "I know I did some terrible things, and I apologize. I know that will never be enough, but it's all I have to offer." Ben has genuine sorrow in his voice, which everyone detects. "But when we win this thing…" Ben begins. "You can all go home to your families and live your lives again."

The crowd looks around at one another trying to figure out what to do next, they appear to believe what he says, but they don't bite the bait. "I'm sorry for what I did okay?" Ben says getting a little rageful. "Just because bad things happened to me didn't give me any good reason to do what I did. I was full of rage, anger, and fear," Ben says continuing to attempt to lift the crowd's spirits. But it isn't going as well as he had hoped.

Shadow Venom

Ben continues to attempt to lift their spirits. "So, in consolation, to say I'm sorry for what I did. If I don't die in the fight…" Ben stutters his way through the sentence. "You can all kill me yourself." The crowd looks around in almost awe. I stand in objection, but it wouldn't matter at this point. The crowd is already throwing their caps into the air. Ben thinks I'm the one with the reformed wicked heart, but after what they just did. I'm not so sure about that. I'm not sure why that makes them so happy. But I know one thing for sure and that's if one of those men dared ask me for help. I'm turning it down. They're more excited about killing my best friend than returning home to their families.

Well, what's left of them anyway.

A faint sound runs across my ear from off in the distance across the bridge. I listen closely again to see if I'm only hearing things, but no. They're here. Everyone readies their stations without making a sound, so we don't alert the enemy. I hide behind the edge of the bridge, out of sight of anyone who may be on the other side of the bridge. Ben tosses me the detonator for the explosives, but I can tell by how he stares at it he regrets handing it over to me.

Jeremiah Anderson

I set the remote down for a moment to tighten my mask, gloves, and anything that needs to be tightened before I rush it to kill everyone I can. Ben snatches the remote out of my hands, and he holds his thumb over the button. I could care less about when it goes off, because it only means that I get to personally give every soldier their ticket to the afterlife.

The Russian soldier's group down at the tip of the bridge, giving Ben the exact opportunity, he wanted. He pushes the button so hard I'm afraid it's going to blow up in his face. Instead, the end of the bridge blows blocking the soldiers from crossing. I leap up from my position and cautiously walk onto the bridge. Ben follows closely behind, but he shakes from the cold breeze.

Ben suddenly stops shaking and walks over to me, placing his hand on my shoulder. "You don't have to become what you dread. This may be my last opportunity to tell you," Ben says releasing his grip on my shoulder and backing up. I grab hold of my shield and clench my fist tightly, readying myself to fight.

The silence almost scares me, causing me to freeze. I don't hear a single gunshot, or any commands to return the attack. The smoke clears away giving me a better view of the end of the bridge, allowing me to see the entire Russian terrorist army standing there as though they think they're too good to attack us. I became irritated with them quickly and signaled to Ben that we needed to move. We ran for the end of the bridge, but as we got closer to the end of the bridge, I saw something small and rounded fly from the trees towards the bridge in front of me. I wonder who would be throwing a pinecone at us. But after a few moments of trying to figure it out, I realize that's not a pinecone. It's a grenade. It impacts with the bridge in front of us blowing up throwing Ben and I off our feet.

My head has a constant pain in it, feeling almost like my brain is trying to escape my skull. A figure appears from the smoke, walking slowly out of it in no rush. He wears a silver helmet that outlines his face, creating a second one on top. With a hood that drapes down the sides of his body, almost thin as paper. He has a shield strapped to his back, and daggers that look to be foot-long blades. But what scares me the most is the large gun he holds.

"These two are mine, kill the rest," the mysterious figure orders.

"Yes, Bane Master. You heard him, fire at will," a soldier calls out from behind the tree line. Bane Master? What's with all the pathetic names that Ben and this guy have been given? I lift myself back onto my feet enough to make it look like my head isn't throbbing in pain. Ben stands up close next to me, gasping for air. I would offer to help him, but I'm pretty sure they don't stop war because someone needs an inhaler.

Bane Master turns to me and gives me a slight groan. "I should have killed you when I had the chance. You, putrid little rodent," Bane Master says. Wait a minute. Should have killed me when he got the chance? Is this… is this Adrick? No, no, no, it can't be. I killed him, right? But then again who else hates me enough to come back from the dead, to give me a one-way ride to the afterlife? It must be him. I can't foresee it being anyone else.

I suppose if I could hit him with a couple of grenades that could fix my problem. I unhook a grenade from my belt, pulling the pin I let the grenade fly. I overshoot it and miss. Adrick comes running, grabbing his large gun from behind his back on a strap. He aims his attention specifically for me. I seem to be a main target of his. Not surprising, since I nearly killed him. Ben fires a few shots of his gun, but Adrick to too fast, he manages to get his shield in time. He's much faster than I remember him, it's insane how fast he's moving. I almost feel as though I have no chance against him. But I beat him last time when the odds were in his favor, now they're in mine.

Adrick looks to be directing his attention over to Ben now. I've felt Adrick's strength, but Ben will not enjoy it. I leap onto Adrick's' back and hold my claws against his neck. I tried to slit his throat, but he has some metal plating from his helmet bleeding down his neck. I won't be able to penetrate it. Adrick throws his hand back behind him and places it on my neck, the pressure nearly knocks me out. Before I can comprehend what's happening, I'm thrown to the ground on my back, confused and unsure of the situation.

I watch as his hand raises in the air ready to finish the kill. I notice how his gloves have sharp points on the ends of his fingers, whilst mine have claws. I brace for the impact of his hand preparing to crush my skull, but nothing happens. I look up and see Ben holding Adrick's hand back, he uses both hands because of Adrick's sheer strength. Adrick grabs hold of one of his knives and swings it at Ben, Ben manages to dodge it. But not without letting go.

Adrick whips back around looking as though he is about to finish me off, but instead, he continues to spin and sweeps Ben's feet from underneath him. Adrick stands back up and stares at Ben before inexplicably bending down and preparing for a jump to land on Ben. I use this as a useful opportunity to regain some time to slow him down. As he leaps into the air, I grab his foot and pull him back to the ground, he smacks on the hard concrete and slams his fist down in anger. I realize that I have to move quickly. I turn over onto my stomach and push myself up off the ground regaining some strength. I stand there for a few moments forgetting what happened, but it all comes back when I feel a hard thump on the back of my head. I fly into the railing on the edge of the bridge and turn myself over to see Adrick holding a dagger in his hand, and him running over to stab me to death.

He swings for my face, but I lock my elbow in his, preventing him from sending the dagger through my skull. I try to hold him off, but I can feel the bones in my arm getting ready to snap because of how much pressure he is using against me. I figure if I can pull my hand over to my right forearm, I might be able to use my flame emitter to push him back from me. I take a deep breath and hope this will work. I release my elbow from his and quickly move my head from where the dagger will land and reach my hand over to my forearm. I turn the flame emitter on and watch as he jumps back from me, giving me much-needed space.

Ben joins in and pushes him back with me, we stand on opposite sides to keep him in check. But I can feel he is about to do something, and I don't like it. I move in closer, but as I do, he throws both his arms toward Ben and me and emits some sort of flame-retardant gas at our flames. He doesn't need to press a button on his arm to activate the gas, instead, he bends his wrists down and that looks to be enough. We move in closer, but Adrick holds his position, as though he doesn't care if he gets burnt to death.

Everything feels to be going well, but that all changes when Adrick turns his attention over to me and ignores Ben. He runs into the flame I sent at him, and still manages to put it out using his spray. He grabs my shirt, lifts me, and throws me into the railing. I manage to maintain my footing, but that doesn't last long. He sends his fist flying into my gut, then gives me a deadly uppercut, and finally sends a strike into the side of my face, causing me to fall onto the ground, dizzy and uncertain whether I will live or not.

His punches, his speed, everything about him has advanced more than the next level. He's almost too strong. He stands over me aiming his gun at my face, I swiftly grab my shield and block every bullet that rains down onto me. Ben stands still, doing nothing. Supposedly trying to figure out what to do.

Ben decides to do it the old-fashioned way, tackling the opponent. They roll over on each other a couple of times before Adrick lands on top and pulls out his daggers. I pulled out mine as well and attacked instinctively. I ran up and gave him a powerful kick to the face, throwing him in the railing. I leap over the railing to stand behind him, pressing my daggers against his chest, and pinning him against the railing. Ben presses his elbow into Adrick's chest, to keep him from moving.

Adrick lets out a loud cough. "I should have killed you, your mother, and your little friend when I had the chance," Adrick says with a voice so raspy I can hardly understand. But what he says shocks me.

Shocks me into realization.

This isn't Adrick. It's Mark. Mark was secretive about why he needed to leave because this is what he was planning on doing. He was able to make it into the Russian prison base uncaptured because he was part of their group. He knew where the enemy was attacking because he was the enemy. He must be one of the Soviet World Condemners. The thought in my mind drives me to fear. Because my real enemy has been with me the whole time.

Anger, hatred, and everything else Ben doesn't want me to become, rushes through my veins. It's all Mark's fault, the pain I feel is his fault. I could have killed him sooner, but I was too stupid to realize it.

My body becomes cold, as though darkness is consuming me. My fists clench tighter around the daggers, and the pressure of the daggers against his chest continues to increase. Until he screams in pain and thrusts himself up from the railing throwing Ben across the bridge.

Anger, hatred, fear, and pain shoot into my veins, allowing me to get the strength I need to… to avenge my father, and the hundreds of innocents. "Oh no," Ben says, aware that I'm about to go insane. I ran like never before, sending a kick to Mark's face, and continuously punching into his gut. The punching doesn't seem to faze him any more than a fly in the face.

Ben jumps back into the fight, giving Mark all, he's got. I try my best to inflect as many of my strongest hand-to-hand combat attacks as possible, but I can't seem to throw anything at him that is strong enough to cause much damage. Enough is enough, I've decided I'm done making this easy on him I need to kill him, no matter the cost. I take a few steps back and pull out my guns.

Before I could pull the trigger, Mark already had his shield out. I sent many bullets to his face, and a few to his body. Not one connects with his body. Ben tries to shoot him as well, but Mark dodges what he can't block. I grow more and more tired of this by the second, so I run up to him ignoring the millions of ways he could kill me. He tries to throw a hook punch at me, but I roll under it before he can hit me.

Ben cups his hands, allowing me to step in them. I put my foot in place and the second I do he throws me into the air. I flip backward until I've landed on Mark's shoulders. I slam my fists in his head and punch him until he gets too angry with me and throws me onto the railing of the bridge for the millionth time.

I stand back up slowly, full of anger. Anger that I'm about to release all over him. "You killed my friends. You killed so many innocents. And you killed my father Now I will get revenge on you for everything you've done," I say running along the railing of the bridge behind him.

"Hunter no!" Ben yells with caution, screaming at the top of his lungs. He must know something I don't, but that doesn't matter because at this point. I'm practically immune to pain. I jump off the railing at Mark. I have my daggers out ready to send into his back. But before I can stab him, Ben runs up to me and shoves me out of the way in midair.

Mark whips around, and in midair, Ben suddenly has a knife stabbed through his chest as though it came from nowhere. Mark slams Ben to the ground and continuously punches him. Ben's goggles smash into pieces, revealing his bloody eyes beneath. Mark stands up, holds Ben by the neck, and faces me. "So, this is the consequence for your sin. He didn't want you to be so rageful, and yet you didn't listen," Mark states. I feel my heart almost stop, with fear. I can't save Ben. My mind feels as though it is melting. My anger and hatred disappeared into a strong sorrow. Mark rips off a small part of Ben's mask around his left eye and strikes Ben's eye with his fist. He sticks his long metal glove fingers into Ben's eye socket, pulls his eye out, holds it in his hand like a trophy, and drops Ben like some rag doll.

My head suddenly gets a huge headache, the pain is unbearable.

Ben was right. He really was right. I thought I could control my anger and use it for what I thought was good. He was right, my anger and hatred did spread, and it did harm others. It killed him. I've been doing this because I was mad because I was in pain. Not because I truly wanted to avenge my father, but because I wanted myself to feel better. I could have focused on saving those I care about, rather than focusing on destroying those that I hate. My hatred has killed Ben, and it is killing me too.

I pull off my mask as it floods with tears. "I'm sorry Ben," I yell loud enough the whole battlefield could hear me, even over the millions of gunshots. "I should have listened to you, I was selfish. I was full of anger and hatred that I couldn't control. It's all my fault," I barely say without choking on tears that find their way into my mouth.

"Ben?" Mark asks with a squeak in his voice. He bends down and pulls off Ben's mask, revealing his face covered in blood. Mark falls to his knees wrapping Ben in his arms and sobbing. I can't help but wonder why he would cry for someone he wanted to kill. Is this guy lost in his mind or something?

Then it hits me. It isn't Mark, It's Mr. Damien. Who else would move so fast, so quick? I don't know why he would try to kill his son and me, but I do know how badly I want to find out.

How could someone be full of so much anger and hatred?

As I am.

Chapter 25

Ben is dead, and his own father Mr. Damien killed him, and it's all my fault. I sold my soul to vengeance, and I paid the price. "How could you do something like this?" I ask though it feels as though I am talking to a blank wall. "To your own son."

He takes off his helmet using a latch in the back, revealing his scared and burnt face. That evil-looking face looks more like a man in pain, a man in need of help. "I didn't want to, they tricked me. They told me they would release my wife and son from capture and pardon us… if I killed you and their Russian traitor. The Dark Condemner," Mr. Damien says. His voice sounds like an old broken record like someone forced him to yell until his vocals broke. Judging by the significant cuts on his neck, they probably tortured him, badly.

Jeremiah Anderson

I don't even know if I should kill him now. He did try to kill me, but does that justify it? Should I kill him to avenge Ben, or would that only lead to anger and hatred? I don't know what's right and what's wrong at this point anymore. I've made too many wrong choices. At this point, I don't know who or what to trust.

I look into Mr. Damien's eyes, and I see a glimpse of something of pure evil. "I suppose I have nothing else to do now..." Mr. Damien starts. "Except kill you. I always finish a job," he says, sending shivers down my spine. I squeeze my fists tightly to prepare for whatever is to come to me next. Mr. Damien rises to his feet, putting his mask back on. He has both daggers in his hand and looking to kill me. The eyes of an evil killer stare into mine, the fear almost controls me. I almost want to turn and run. All the soldiers behind me have risked their lives for me, so everyone can avenge their loved ones. But I'm the only one that took anger out on my enemy. And got someone that I care about killed.

I look up and the sky has turned into a bleak and dark grey. There is thunder so loud that it pounds my eardrums, and the lightning is bright enough to blind me. Red lights are shining in the sky causing the clouds to have a glowing red color and the lightning to become a bright sinister red color. The rain comes down and hits hard. Feeling as though cement is hitting me in the face.

Mr. Damien stands in front of me shaking in pure anger. With a hatred that I once knew. A hatred that got my best friend killed. His clothes are stained with blood from where Ben and I scratched him, and they have holes in them from possible bullet holes. I look down at my own clothes and my hands are bloody and my whole body aches and blood dripping from where I was cut.

I almost forget where I am until a man runs towards me. Mr. Damien. I grab hold of my shield and hold it in front of my body as he throws the daggers at my chest. There are a few moments of silence until my shield is ripped from my hands and lifted high above me. I roll out of the way just as the edge of the shield is about to come in contact with me. Judging by the sound of the impact against the bridge, that impact would have probably chopped me in half. My back gets a sudden pain, I try to think about what it could be, but that's when I remember. My katana. I pull it out and swing it at Mr. Damien's legs. It might not be able to do anything to him, but it might be enough to annoy him. Maybe I don't have to kill anyone, I only need to stop him enough to prevent him from killing anyone. However, with someone like this, that seems to be quite impossible. But I'll try for Ben.

Blinking for only a moment. I lose track of Mr. Damien. I look around and can't find him anywhere. But I find him when I feel a crushing pressure around my neck that picks me up and throws me against the bridge. The consistent being thrown against the bridge causes me to almost black out. But I'm snapped out of it when a punch is sent to my gut. I feel nauseous, and unsure whether this is a fight I can win. He's like me but faster, stronger, bigger, and much more powerful than I could wish to be, not to mention more experienced.

"I'm sorry Ben," I say, before savoring every last breath I can get.

Mr. Damien releases his grip on me. Allowing me to escape from him. "Never say his name. You have no right," he yells to me. I can still barely understand him from his raspy voice. Before I know it, I'm slammed to the ground. I try to reach for something, but I can't. It's too far. Mr. Damien cocks his gun. Pointing it to my head, I have nothing else I can do. I closed my eyes to accept my fate, but then I heard a gunshot.

I'm still alive?

Shadow Venom

I open my eyes and see the Strike Back Stingers moving in, firing their guns at Mr. Damien. For a brief moment I felt as though we might win, but I know that's not so. Those men just gave up their lives for mine, because the moment they fired those bullets, that was it for them.

Mr. Damien uses Ben's shield and his own to block the incoming bullets. He runs up to the soldiers, deflects their guns away from him using the shields, and grabs hold of the barrels. They wear no helmets, so I can see the looks on their faces when Mr. Damien pulls the gun out of one of the soldiers' hands and hits him on the head with the gun knocking him over. The other soldier fires his gun and tries to take control of it using both hands. But Mr. Damien uses only one hand to knock the gun back into the soldier's face, causing the firing bullets to go into the soldier's head. Killing him in only a matter of seconds.

After killing that one soldier Mr. Damien turns to the other soldier, laying on the ground helplessly. Mr. Damien grabs his gun from the strap around his back and fires into the soldier's body until he appears to be dead. Another soldier attacks from behind, but Mr. Damien must have suspected this because he turns around and immediately sends the dagger the soldier holds, into his neck.

Another soldier attacks, and another, and another after that. They endlessly try to stop Mr. Damien until there is nothing left but a bunch of dead bodies left on the ground. Finally, when I feel I might have enough energy to fight. I consider standing, but gravity still feels like it wants to pull me back down to earth. Mr. Damien walks slowly in my direction, then suddenly falls to the ground. I look to see what might have caused it, and I see one last Strike Back Stinger behind him. It's that stuck-up guy who only used a shield. I thought that I had killed him. He still uses only a shield. Despite him being very fast and strong, he is no match for Mr. Damien. Then again. He did want a challenge.

Mr. Damien jumps back at him, but the guy manages to move out of the way in time. Lucky. He goes in for a punch, but Mr. Damien moves like a cheetah and catches the punch before it can even get close to hitting him. He sweeps the guy off his feet and slams him to the ground. The guy knows what is about to happen next and accepts it. Mr. Damien raises a shield above his head and sends it into the guy's face. Ending his life.

Shadow Venom

After sending a few bullets into the guy to make sure he's dead. Mr. Damien turned his attention to me. Walking back over to stand in front of me in the same position we were in only a few minutes ago. He points his gun to my head again and eagerly pulls the trigger. I hear a click, but no shot. He's out of bullets. I roll out of the way to pick up a gun lying on the ground and hold it in my hands ready for use.

End this. Now. My mind keeps telling me. Is this the right thing to do? I don't know what is right or wrong anymore. That evil and anger within me is trying to control me. But I won't let it. Ben was right. Hatred is not the answer. I need to at least try and let Mr. Damien live. Hold him off. Until I can separate right from wrong. I'm not going to make any life-altering choices like that. No matter if it costs my life.

I chose to fire a shot at his gun causing a small explosion, sending us both flying in separate directions. "Never mind the gun. I wanted to kill you myself anyways," Mr. Damien states with pure hatred in his voice. I ran at him and sent a few kicks to his face and chest. They don't do much but give me an opening to pull off some of his armor. He doesn't even care to stop me from pulling off his armor, he just goes for my neck again. He is completely predictable. I put that knowledge to good use. Even with his hand on my throat I leap onto the railing of the bridge and flip off it which releases his grip on me. He tries to stab me again with his daggers. Every attack I survive. And counter it with something stronger.

His anger fuels him. It causes him to be much more insane. But because of it. In reality, it is weakening him. Before my attacks wouldn't do anything to him. But now because he isn't in his right mind, he is only trying to seek revenge. It's destroying him. This must have been what Ben was seeing in me.

And he was right.

I jump onto Mr. Damien and rest on his shoulders long enough to unlatch his Mask from his head. I land on the ground and throw it into the river below. He tries to hit me again, but it seems as though I'm getting faster. I grab hold of his hood and rip it off him. Exposing his scared head, with him being burnt from behind his left ear creeping its way to the whole left side of his head. I didn't get as good a look before. I rise holding a gun in my hand and carefully point it in his direction. Deciding to drop it almost instantly I remembered that I didn't want to kill him. Instead, I pick up a shield and hold it up. He picks up a few large guns the soldiers used and sends every bullet my way.

Shadow Venom

I tried to push forward to stop his gunfire, but the strength of the gunfire continued to push me back. I begin to feel the bullets hitting my shield as they begin to push through it. Breaking it. I see cracks from the edges of the shield leading into the center of it. The ends are sharp and broken, whilst the rest of the shield has holes that continue to dig deeper inside of it until they start to fly out the other side. I expect it to break into a million pieces at any moment. I rolled away right as a large missile flew my way that the Russians tried to hit me with. Instead, it makes an impact on the other side of the river, blowing up a good number of soldiers on my side.

My breath grows so heavy, soon I can barely stand. Has he stabbed me? Shot me? What has happened? It takes a few moments to figure it out, but that's when I realize what the problem is. I'm fighting Mr. Damien. I can't do this anymore. He can attack me all he wants, but it isn't going to affect how I am going to react. Sometimes the best thing to do is nothing. I don't know what the best thing is anymore, so I'm willing to suffer to figure that out.

If I can keep him busy long enough; I will save the lives of millions of people. I just can't let him have the opportunity to fight my men.

Jeremiah Anderson

I dropped all my weight and let myself drop to the ground. Perhaps he may self-destruct, or maybe while he's using me as a punching bag, my guys can hurry up and win this thing. Before Mr. Damien kills me of course.

I am picked up and thrown across the bridge, no different than all the other times. "It's all your fault," Mr. Damien says fighting back tears. "He's dead because of you. If you could've controlled yourself, he might still be alive. But no, you wanted revenge. Because you couldn't control yourself. You should have been the one to die. Not him," he says looking at me with such hatred, such evil. He has so much determination to kill me that he could probably do it by simply wishing so. He's so blinded that he doesn't even realize he's the one who truly killed him, but he's also not wrong. Ben wouldn't have had to save me if I would've controlled myself.

"Not him!" Mr. Damien says as he charges at me. I consider trying to stop him. But if he wants me to suffer, that means he won't kill me yet, so I will have to simply endure the pain until the end. I am lifted from the ground and placed on the railing of the bridge. He smashes down on my chest like he is trying to start my lungs, instead he's attempting to stop them. I refuse to fight back. The pain is excruciating. I may not even be making the right choice but, it's the one I want to make.

320

Shadow Venom

Mr. Damien grabs my calves and throws me back onto the hard cement of the bridge. He punches me in the face with everything he's got. I can feel every inch of my skull breaking. He slams his elbow against my ribs constantly. I can feel that he has broken my ribs.

After taking many punches I realize that I don't need to be giving hits, nor do I necessarily need to take them. I can try to at least dodge his attack. I need to hold him off as long as I can, so the Americans can win against the Russians. I try to think of a way to get him off me, then that's when I remember. My electrified venom shocker. I quickly turn it on, with it being the only thing I can hold him off with, it better work. He doesn't seem to notice or care, so I don't hesitate to send a punch right into his chest, making him fly back across the bridge. I could easily kill him, but all I need to do is keep him at bay, so it needs to be on low enough of a setting to push him back but not kill him.

He gets back up. And charges at me again.

So, I sent another punch at him.

So, he gets up again.

Jeremiah Anderson

And I hit him again.

Every time I punch him and cause him to fly across the bridge he only gets back up and tries to attack me again. He isn't trying to attack me in any other way. He's lost his ability to reason with himself. He refuses to do anything else. He continues to try hand-to-hand combat because he wants to kill me so badly. He can't think of a more awful way to do it. I continue to send shocks of electricity into his body, each time causing him to become more irritated and irrational with himself.

He's lost all reason with himself and the outside world. He has been truly corrupted by evil within. And the hatred that breeds that evil and anger.

He runs at me once more in an attempt to kill me. I pulled my arm back ready to send another punch into his chest. He soon is in reach of my punch, so I send one his way. But this one didn't blast him back. Shivers go up my spine as he sends a punch into my face. The punch pushes me significantly back but doesn't take me down. Mr. Damien sends another punch into my gut, and another across my face, and another, and another.

Until I feel as though I can't take much more.

Shadow Venom

He grabs my shoulder and leans in close to me to give a few punches to my ribs. I scream in anguish from the pain. It's like he's been going easy on me this entire time. What if he delivers a full-force punch? Every punch up to this point has been pulled. I breathe heavier than I ever have before.

Fear is overcoming me, but I know I cannot let it.

Mr. Damien releases me from his grasp. For an instant trust him. But before I could comprehend what happened, I got swept off my feet. Then caught again in his arms and slammed into the railing. He puts tremendous pressure on my back, reassuring me that I won't escape.

He grabs the back of my head with one hand and the other is used the press down on me.

"Look at them," Mr. Damien says. I try to turn my head away, but he forces it back in place. "You could have saved them, but instead you're going to die. You all will," he doesn't even realize that the Russians will eventually kill him, they don't want anyone to escape and leak their secrets. He's killing himself and he doesn't even realize it.

Jeremiah Anderson

The rain falls into my mouth and eyes. Stinging my skin on contact. My lungs burn from the cold, and my fingers steadily shake trying to warm themselves up. The lightning flashes and burns my eyes.

Everything freezes for a couple of moments, as I hear American soldiers yelling to other soldiers to tell their family members that they love them, and to avenge their sacrifice, as they attempt to swim across the river and carry grenades and other explosives to the other side. Some make it, but most do not. I hear the screams of those who get shot and are dragged back away from the battlefield. Some are shot and helplessly sink from wounds in the water. They will likely drown.

I'm snapped back to reality when Mr. Damien puts even more pressure on me. "You were always like a second son to me." His voice almost has a hint of kindness. But that quickly fades. "Now fight me," he says, acting as though this is some game. He treats me as though he can get into my head and defeat me that way.

But no.

Not anymore.

"I won't fight anymore. I give up," I said. If I can overload his brain, cause him to go crazy enough. I just might be able to win that way.

"Fight me now!" he yells louder, loud enough the entire battlefield could hear.

"I... I will n... never fight you as long as I live." I'm barely able to get a sentence out, but it's enough to cause him to become even more frustrated with me.

"Fine then. I guess I'll have to prevent you from fighting for the rest of your life, which shouldn't be much longer," he lifts me by my right calf and raises me above the edge of the bridge upside down. This is my time... to die. I've accepted defeat, I may bleed out and drown in that river, but at least I'll be in belief that I did the right thing in the end.

He pulls out his dagger and holds it to my stomach. There is nothing else I can do at this point, using my other leg to kick him wouldn't help me any, we both would fall into the river and I'm too weak to fight back against the current.

Jeremiah Anderson

"For you Ben," he mutters while choking back tears. He pulls the dagger closer to his chest. I watch as he takes a deep breath and begins to swing his dagger. He unexpectedly swings it not for my gut, but for my calf. He slices right through my right calf, causing me to fall as my foot is being held in his hand. I think fast and grab hold of the railing on the bridge, and dangle on that. I try to pull myself up, but I can't. My arms can barely grip on.

"Aah!" I scream in pain. The pain is unbearable, it's the worst physical pain that I've ever had to deal with. Blood drips from my leg and into the water below. I feel dizzy, and I am starting to lose consciousness. I can't fight back.

"This is for your own good Hunter, and for the good of everyone else," Mr. Damien says looking down from above me. He lifts his dagger high, ready to send it into my fingers to stop me from having any chance of living.

I accept my fate. That this is the end.

Suddenly.

A bright light shines behind Mr. Damien. At first, I thought it was my gateway to heaven. Then I realized it was a helicopter, with a soldier inside manning a large gun. I look closer to see if they're on our side. I can barely make out a figure, but it's Mark. Mark came to save me.

I never doubted him for a second.

Mr. Damien turns around to meet his fate. The only thing I can see is Mr. Damien moving closer to the helicopter out of my line of sight. The pain in my leg is excruciating and awful. I figure if Mr. Damien is defeated, then my work is done. Plus, with a helicopter on our side now. We can't lose. So, it's time for me to meet my fate. I take a deep breath and let go of the bridge.

I plummeted into the water below.

The blood from my legs slithers out like a snake in the water, floating away. I look around at the light around me, and I say goodbye to it.

Because this may be the last time that I see it.

I have been given what I deserve.

Jeremiah Anderson
<u>Epilogue</u>

I thought I was going to die. The first night of me playing Shadow Venom of course. I believed that I was doing the right thing from the beginning. I thought that I was right for bottling up that anger and hatred and evil inside of me to release on my enemy. But the truth is my real enemy was myself. I caused the death of my best friend Ben. The truth is he didn't die because of the Dark Condemner, it was me who killed him. It's my fault. I wish I could undo what I did, but I can't. It's already been done. Looking back, I probably should have killed Bane Master, but I didn't. That's because I didn't want it to be out of anger. So, if I can say anything of importance while I'm up here, then that's if you want to accomplish something or avenge someone. Do it because you love your friend, not because you hate your enemy.

This is what I say as I stand at a podium in front of thousands of people in my town of Forest Hills. They all look at each other, deciding whether to worship me, because I saved them. Or to fear me because of what I've done. I try to stand using a crunch the doctors gave me after they found me in the water. The one leg I have left now has to support my whole body.

Things certainly will never be the same.

But that's okay. Because if things were the same then I would never learn.

I look behind my back and give a small smile to the three people I chose to be on stage with me. My mother, Chloe, and Mark. I stared at them for a couple moments.

But then something changed. The air almost tastes bitter.

Something isn't good. I can sense it.

My friends and family look appalled and all stare off in the same direction. It isn't until Mark is shot in the chest that I turn my head to find Mr. Damien standing up on stage with a trail of dead bodies behind him. I stare at him as he shoots everyone that was behind me on stage.

I don't look to see who. Since I'm too appalled in fear.

He then turns his attention to me. I was shot in my one good leg, then in my arm. I don't feel any of it because of the adrenaline that is shooting through my veins. He raises his gun aiming for my face, and a couple of men

grab him to try and save me, but not soon enough.

He pulls the trigger.

Everything goes black… I'm dead.

End Of Book One

Shadow Venom

Acknowledgments

I would like to thank everyone who has contributed to the creative process in the creation of my book.

Gabe. Thank you for being my friend and convincing me that this dream was possible. I wouldn't have ever thought this would happen without you. Thank you for giving me the mindset to accomplish my childhood dream.

Dad. Thank you for believing in me and supporting the choices that I make even if you don't always agree with them. I will never forget how you've been my biggest supporter in my authoring career so far. Especially thank you for teaching me the value of family and for teaching me right and wrong.

Grandma. Thank you. It means so much to me that you took the time to help me come up with the book cover for **Shadow Venom**. It looks absolutely fantastic, and I will think about you every time that I look at it. Your creative abilities are something truly special.

Mom. Thank you for helping me achieve my goal of writing my book by helping me to earn money to publish this book. I can never express the happiness that it has brought me. Your kind and tenderheartedness are what inspired Hunter's mother in my book.

Ms. Flint. Thank you so much for being my first reader and giving me so much good advice on how to improve my book. I will continue to use the skills of what you have taught me to improve myself in my future literary works.

I've appreciated having you all in my journey to becoming an author, and I hope that I can bless you as much as you've blessed me.

Shadow Venom

About the Author

Jeremiah Anderson is the author of the novel *Shadow Venom*. Though he did not have much experience in the publishing world, he was only sixteen at the time when he published his book. He enjoys books with a little mystery as well as exciting twists. He plans to write many more books for his authoring career.

Shadow Venom

www.ingramcontent.com/pod-product-compliance
Lightning Source LLC
Chambersburg PA
CBHW071848220626
47052CB00002B/19